ALSO BY ARI NEWMAN

Mrs. Vanderbilt

AMERICA FIRST A Modern Fable

The Mueller Report Uncertainty

AMERICA FIRST

A Modern Fable

Special Impeachment Edition

ARI NEWMAN

AMERICA FIRST A Modern Fable
Special Impeachment Edition

All Rights Reserved
Copyright © 2020 Ari Newman
Edited by Dianne Z. Newman

A derivative work of the screenplay
STATE OF THE UNION Copyright © 2007 Ari Newman
The Library of Congress has catalogued the U.S. edition as follows:
Copyright Registration Number: PAu003078040
ISBN: 978-0-9986672-9-4

Published By
Mrs. Vanderbilt Novel LLC
First Edition Published 2017
Second Edition Published 2020
WRITTEN IN JERUSALEM ISRAEL
PUBLISHED IN THE UNITES STATES OF AMERICA

To Mom and Dad,
I love you so much

CONTENTS

INTRODUCTION

Post Impeachment

The date is January 31, 2020 and tomorrow Donald Trump will be acquitted in his Impeachment and the next Maximilien Robespierre will be born.

Senators, you are the victims of a narcissist. You are questioning the fragility before you not because you want to do that which is right and just, but because you don't know how.

As a guide to this special printing of this fictional book there are two essays. The first is UNCERTAINTY – A Treatise on the Victims of Political Narcissism which was published May 9 2019 as part of the book The Mueller Report Uncertainty www.TheMuellerReportBook.com. The second is UNMASKING The Trump Responsa.

PREFACE

I began to convert my screenplay into a book on Sunday morning, January 22, 2017 after experiencing the events in Washington D.C. and around the world during the previous 48 hours. I originally planned to spend the day enjoying some NFL football.

The screenplay was originally written in 2006 after hearing the then unknown state senator Barack Obama say these words, "to slice-and-dice our country into Red States and Blue States; Red States for Republicans, Blue States for Democrats...there is not a liberal America and a conservative America — there is the United States of America. There is not a black America and a white America and Latino America and Asian America — there's the United States of America."

My partners and I were about to produce the film having received a preliminary green-light from the first studio that read it. We were assigned an account executive and everything was moving ahead until everything in Hollywood stopped due to the Writer's Guild strike. Within several weeks, the project's account executive along with thousands of others' jobs had been lost; it took years for the motion picture industry to recover while simultaneously experiencing a deflating DVD market and the Great Recession. Those who have enjoyed HBO's *Entourage* or have screened the films *The Player* or Kevin Bacon's *The Big Picture* realize that this type of scenario is very common in the motion picture business. Like everybody else, we moved on with other projects knowing that we could always pull it off the shelf. With Obama's presidency attempting to tackle the Red State / Blue State divide, the time wasn't right for this storyline.

Two final thoughts - Since this book was adapted from a screenplay it is written in a simple and easy to understand manner. While the story addresses complex issues related to government and politics (hopefully to be enjoyed by all regardless of political ideology) it is not filled with fancy wording or with the intention of being the best fable ever written. For this reason, it is perfect for younger readers (14 and up i.e. "PG-13") who might not be the best readers (I wasn't at that age) or for those where English is a second language to improve reading comprehension and/or to initiate discussion and healthy debate about government, American history, political science, etc. Finally, and for me perhaps the most important, I want to use this opportunity to thank everyone from near and far for their support and encouragement and for those who believed in me even when I didn't believe in myself.

Please feel welcome to post any comments or thoughts you may have about the book or any topic or theme political, literary, or whatever...

Dedicated to those who feel that they don't have a voice – you do and you are not alone.

Poet Danny Siegel teaches that when W.H. Auden was asked about the meaning of his poetry he said, "My poetry never saved a child from Auschwitz."

FORWARD

History repeats itself as we are again in danger of moving from terrorism to war, The Third Great War. The causes of the Second World War combined with the reasons the Central Powers lost World War I are precisely what has and is now happening.

Barbara Tuchman outlined how the stage was set for the Great War with the funeral of Edward VII and a conflict that began brewing among three cousins: the King, the Kaiser and the Tzar. The Schlieffen plan was doomed to fail not only because it was outdated, but once Germany found itself trapped in a trench warfare stalemate, the plan did not account for a war of attrition. Although the assassination of Archduke Franz Ferdinand triggered the honoring of alliance treaties which ultimately led to World War I, it was lost due to a flawed strategy, unachievable operational goals, and poor tactics.

The Second Great War became a question of "when" and not "if" when experts in war planning, personified by the fictitious character Pug Henry in Herman Wouk's "The Winds of War" challenged conventional wisdom by advising FDR that Poland would be next, after the German/Russian proxy war in Spain during its revolution, Japan's invasion of China, and most significant, Chamberlain's appeasement of Hitler after Germany annexed Austria and the Sudetenland. Subsequently, when Germany breached the Munich Agreement, a vacuum was created in Czechoslovakia allowing its neighbors to grab disputed territory. Pug Henry predicted that although Polish independence would be guaranteed by Britain and France, Hitler would not be deterred; then in September 1939, using the pretext of Polish aggression, Germany invaded Poland leading to World War II.

The stage was set for the Third Great War when American and its Western allies removed the Iraqi army from Kuwait. For the first time since the Versailles Treaty, the Allies put hundreds of thousands of troops on the ground to redraw and control the map of ancient Mesopotamia. Although Iraq was repelled, the Bush Plan created many more problems than it solved, and its ultimate failure led to two falling dominoes: First, in the Muslim world the Salafists, Wahhabis, and others gained legitimacy with groups like Al-Qaida, and second, a decade later Bush the Son, considered by many on the streets in the Arab world to be his father's heir, would invade Iraq using the false pretext that it was retaliation for the 911 attacks. While Baghdad quickly fell, the war was lost because Bush held an outdated view of the role of mass media and never took into account the importance of social media and all that it would reveal. Abu Ghraib, the failed policy of de-baathification, and the weapons of mass destruction fiasco all led to decreasing support for the war in America and amongst her Allies, attrition amongst the troops, and the deaths of hundreds of thousands of people causing an insurgency and a Sunni/Shia military conflict. After a civil war in Iraq, the Allies eventually withdrew, the Arab Spring flourished, ISIS filled the vacuum, the Russians annexed Crimea (and very recently became the de facto protector of President Assad of Syria), and in other parts of the old Ottoman Empire from Tunis and Libya to Syria and Turkey there was yet another "land grab" by newly created alliances and rulers leading to World War III. Once again eroding support due to decades of a flawed strategy resulting in a "land grab", Bush W's unachievable operational goals, and poor tactics are creating a "perfect storm" mirroring the errors of the loosing sides in the first two World Wars.

Is it comforting to know that this Third Great War, like the others, will eventually end? Perhaps, though viewed more cynically, the cycle will unfortunately repeat, and there will be a Fourth Great War, a fifth, a sixth and so on, easily predictable because old men have always found a way to get young people to fight for them.

It is because he read Barbara Tuchman's book, *The Guns of August*, and learned from history's mistakes, that John F. Kennedy was able to (and credited his ability to) avoid triggering a Third Great War in 1962 over Cuba. And so it is with his words that is the Epilogue of America First? Which One?

J. Rambler Perkins

January 2017

PROLOGUE

In 1990 during the Presidency of George H.W. Bush then Secretary of Defense Dick Cheyney received a top secret report of the three most likely military threats to the United States. The third most likely was an incident with North Korea; the second most likely was that Saddam Hussein would invade Kuwait; and the most likely was a nuclear attack on the World Trade Center and Wall Street to incapacitate the American financial market. Several months later Saddam Hussein invaded Iraq.

The reason President Bush and Vice President Dick Cheyney testified before the 9/11 Commission in secret and not under oath or on the record was not to protect Bush, but to protect Cheyney.

UNCERTAINTY

Special Impeachment Edition

A Treatise on the Victims of Political Narcissism

I HAVE RESOLVED TO MAKE these introductory statements, and in deed those of the entire book, easy and accessible, rather than difficult and remote, by citing the fundamentals of the proofs and arguments and not their detailed implications, so that readers may find their way about without too much difficulty. By making their study straightforward, they will attain their object, which is justice and truth." - Saadia Gaon (10th Century Philosopher).

In the heart of the holy city of Jerusalem, Israel on the Sabbath I sit in my seat at Congregation Moreshet Yisrael across the street from the official Prime Minister's Residence and recently I have found myself drifting from the weekly teachings of the Bible or the sermon being delivered from the pulpit to reading Saadia Gaon's most famous work, *The Book of Belief and Opinions*.

It was originally written in Judeo-Arabic (Arabic words written in Hebrew letters) and has been translated by only a handful of scholars over the last millennia. Even in English, it is not an easy read and the philosophical narratives are complex but once understanding begins to take shape it is as rewarding as hearing the answers to those universal questions (which are too often the rationalization for belief or religious practice) of where we came from, what happens when we die, and who is G-d. These truths arise from an understanding of what is seemingly uncertain and therefore unexplainable.

To accomplish this Saadia Gaon does not attempt to circumvent the inconsistencies of faith and science, but he positions in parallel the truths of revelation adjacent to rationale thought and intertwines them in a labyrinth of observations that, "many of the faithful lack pure convictions and possess mistaken convictions, while many of the deniers boast of their corruption and act haughtily towards the men of truth, although they are themselves in error," leaving the inverse as truth.

The uncertainty we will be studying here is how can we be victims of something we cannot see, touch, understand or even believe exists. In this case it is Donald Trump's Narcissistic Personality Disorder (in this work "Narcissism" will be the term used) that is our subject. Specifically it is not does he suffer from it (as that is medically not in dispute) but how can we have missed it since only once we understand its complexities can we begin to accept ourselves as victims without shame and take appropriate action thereafter. In an attempt to explain that which seems unknowable (narcissism in this case) I am offering Saadia Gaon's technique in tackling this subject through proving truths using the uncertainties surrounding it.

What are we uncertain about? Does Trump have narcissism and how do we exist with such a truth? Who are the victims and what is next for them? By simple definition narcissism is a fraud and one who suffers from it is a fraudster or con-artist or worse. [Remember and importantly so that narcissism is not something we chose it is something we are born with as examined later in this text.] If it is fact that should any candidate suffer from such an affliction would cause him not be eligible to become or ever elected to be the President of the United States then this matter is of primary national concern. How could we all have been fooled? What is it that almost everybody doesn't see? We would not have elected a convicted robber or fraudster so what error did we make here?

Briefly using Saadia Gaon's philosophy, the central question is what causes errors in "man" (a term for better or worse I will use to mean both man and woman as I will be using "he" a great deal in this text) which in this example of NPD prevented us from identifying it right before us in plain sight. The answer is when intelligibles are based upon sensibles -- Intelligibles being the object and content of the intellect and sensibles being the object and content of our senses.

The Object in this case it narcissism itself and its Content are the traits, and the analysis thereof, by which narcissism manifests itself. According to the American Psychiatric Association's Diagnostic and Statistical Manual of Mental Disorders, Fifth Edition (DSM-5) narcissism is defined as comprising a pervasive pattern of grandiosity (in fantasy or behavior), a constant need for admiration, and a lack of empathy, beginning by early adulthood and present in a variety of contexts, as indicated by the presence of at least 5 of the following 9 criteria:

1. A grandiose sense of self-importance
2. A preoccupation with fantasies of unlimited success, power, brilliance, beauty, or ideal love
3. A belief that he or she is special and unique and can only be understood by, or should associate with, other special or high-status people or institutions
4. A need for excessive admiration
5. A sense of entitlement
6. Interpersonally exploitive behavior
7. A lack of empathy
8. Envy of others or a belief that others are envious of him or her
9. A demonstration of arrogant and haughty behaviors or attitudes

What has caused people to either not question or understand narcissism in Donald Trump is that doubts may arise concerning proofs "apprehended by sense through one of two causes: either because the person who is inquiring has an inadequate idea of the object of the investigation, or because he is casual and perfunctory in his observation and research. Take the case of a person who is looking for John Doe. He maybe in doubt whether he has found him for one of two reasons: either because his knowledge of John Doe is inadequate, since he never met him before and therefore does not know him, or because he may casually assume that some other person that he sees is John Doe. By taking matters lightly, and neglecting to make proper inquiries, he seeks him half-heartedly and with little application. He will never recognize him." In this case the "Trump Supporter" doesn't understand NPD so can therefore not recognize and should such a person knew what to look for he was casual in his inquiry so that such proof would never be achieved

"We can say the same for the things apprehended by our intellect. Here again doubts arise from one of two causes: either because the person who seeks intellectual knowledge is unfamiliar with the methods of demonstration – he judges a bad proof to be correct, and a good one, incorrect –or he knows the right methods of investigation, but he treats the matter lightly and carelessly, rushing to a conclusion about some object of knowledge before having completed the art of investigation concerning it. The case is worse when both deficiencies are combined in the same person, that is to say, when the person is not acquainted with the art of investigation and, in addition, lacks patience to achieve what he can truly know about his object of inquiry. He will remain far removed from that object, and will despair of attaining it." In this case even if the "Trump Supporter" could spot a person with NPD the lack of methodology of seeking proof or process of examining the Contents (i.e. traits as stated above) would not allow him to reach such a conclusion – he knows where he's going but doesn't know how to get there.

"The case is still worse when we add to these deficiencies a third, namely, that the inquirer has no clear idea as to what he really wishes to know. Then he is so removed from attaining true knowledge that, even if the truth should chance upon him, he would not notice it." In my view, this is not an example of the average "Trump Supporter" as they would fall into the first two categories. Rather, this is a category in which I would place Mitch McConnell, Sarah Sanders, and Sean Hannity. Yes, like the Trump Supporter they are victims and in their specific cases they should know better but the narcissist can keep those around him with no clear idea of what they wish to know. They are consumed with themselves and so removed by their inner agenda that should Trump be "Unmasked" (a term explained later), either by his own doing or a result of the inevitable, they wouldn't notice it – and if they don't notice it they couldn't accept it.

Lastly (and this is something that has bothered me for some time), since I don't know where else to put this in the text I will just state it here. In my non-medical opinion I believe the reason why Trump sometimes stumbles over his words is because he suffers from mild dyslexia. Again, this is something that he was born with and was probably never properly diagnosed and therefor never treated. There is nothing wrong with dyslexia (it is not as if the person did something wrong) and we probably all know people who have it many of whom have overcome the symptoms. My politics have nothing to do with the subject of this text and while making fun of Trump's policies or even mannerisms on late night TV is funny I think we should lay off the dyslexia. There is plenty of material to begin with and we all have disabilities and limitations and would not like it if others made fun of us.

♦ ♦ ♦

I have had several encounters with a narcissist; one with whom I worked, who won a gated, who I created as a character in my book Mrs. Vanderbilt, and one we see on TV every day. The narcissist does not realize that he is one. He simply believes he is normal and everyone is like- Much in the same way a person who is colorblind believes that all people see colors as he does but for someone telling him. Could one who was colorblind become a successful painter? Of course, so long as one understands that when he sees blue it is really green. The narcissist is the same. Although it is very uncommon, if he understand that he's narcissism not normal he can overcome how it manifests itself even though there is no cure. Without understanding that he is a narcissist and by not seeking appropriate therapy success in life, love, work, and happiness for the narcissist is extremely unlikely.

A conclusion can therefore be reached that although the word itself a sounds "evil," A narcissist can in fact achieve greatness in society and live a righteous life. Taking this idea to illogical extreme is to simply examine history's most evil individual, Adolf Hitler. Hitler was not a narcissist – evil, yes. This conclusion can be understood because he tried to hide his crimes. He knew what he was doing in Auschwitz and the other camps were crimes of genocide. Alternatively, a narcissist would not have any reason to hide his crime as he does not see his actions as criminal. Ironically, one might make the argument that General Patton was a narcissist (using "Fauxpology" as described in the Glossary), yet he was loved by the men he commanded, is credited with defeating General Rommel in North Africa and famously saved the 101st Airborne division in the Battle of the Bulge. What made Patton a great general however was that he knew he was seen as an ass and a *prima donna*. General Eisenhower was able to use this Patton quality to the Allies' advantage most notably in the preparation for D-Day by tricking Hitler to believe the invasion would be commanded by Patton and the target would be the Pas de Calais rather than Normandy.

As stated there is no cure for narcissism and there is no way to prevent it. Although there has been little study about narcissism it is widely believed to be hereditary, progress of the more prevalent with age, and either enhanced or limited by environment. The actions of a narcissist it's statistically predictive. For example, much in the way that there are not many 70 year old American football players, coal workers, and drug users walking around, the same is true of narcissists. Throughout his life the narcissist will have trouble holding a job, finding or maintaining a home, and staying married or in a committed relationship. For some odd reason I have noticed that many professional successful narcissists gravitate to the real estate industry. Regardless of industry or circumstance one can easily get what one wants from the narcissist if, and only if, you know that they are a full blown narcissist. This does not apply to a person that shows narcissistic trends for behavior since in the make-up of our egos we all enjoy one or two narcissistic attributes. This is why it is called Narcissistic Personality Disorder. It is the personality that is germane not just the behavior.

Unfortunately Trump's narcissism is so pervasive and therefore extremely predictable and transparent. Why?

First, assume that the subject is lying and the more comfortable he appears the more he is lying. Therefore simple understanding that whatever the narcissist is stating believe that the opposite is true. The narcissist will stay with the lie even if they are faced with the truth. A normal person would admit the lie and feel shame and apologize whereas the narcissist will not only enhance the lie but will introduce new lies and severely criticize the person confronting them with the truth. For example, when he was caught in the "Hurricane Dorian Sharpie" lie and then doubled down on his lie. In fact, the narcissist can be so convincing of the lie and his reprimand of us for not seeing truth the way he does (despite truth and fact) that we start believing the narcissist and see the lie as truth.

Second, assume that the subject will not finish what they start. It is the constant starting of something new and announcing it that the narcissist crave while completing a task is of little interest because once the high of the announcement and admiration wear off the narcissist has already moved on to something new to achieve the same or greater high.

Third, those that the narcissist belittles and makes jokes about are those who the narcissist is most afraid of and / or envious of.

In summary lies, jealousy, and follow thru. To illustrate this let's examine North Korea and Kim Jong-un as they were able to identify Trump as a narcissist and use it against him in their dealings with the United States and the civilized world.

- Lie – Trump talking tough about using military force against North Korea. Opposite – Trump was never going to use military force.
- Envy / Jealousy – Trump calling Kim Jong-un "Rocket Man" demonstrates his envy of the North Korean leader.
- Follow Thru – Starting "talks" with the North Koreans with no interest, or for that matter ability, to reach an agreement. This allowed the North Korean government to take a victory lap in the eyes of the world leaders albeit by all accounts their nuclear activities appear to continue.

Putin, Macron, and Netanyahu have all been able to manipulate Trump to get what they want. Putin because Trump is afraid of him, Macron because in one act he fed Trump's ego and caused Trump to be envious of him with his Bastille Day Military Parade, and Netanyahu because he got

Trump to do politically what other Presidents wouldn't so that Trump could claim he was the "first president to do it" and the "best friend of Israel". Netanyahu was also smart enough to understand that Trump would announce the "best peace plan ever," while the Prime Minister recognized that either a peace plan would never be proposed or that he could allow Trump to declare little victories one at a time. For example moving the embassy to Jerusalem, recognizing the Golan Heights, and (at the time of writing this on April 10, 2019 the morning after Netanyahu was likely re-elected) annexing the West bank. In totality Trump would declare peace and brag about how he did it and then belittle those in the Palestinian leadership as Terrorists or Iranian agents.

Examining Trumps other major lies can reveal his true intentions.

1. A great health plan, "the best ever," means he has no plan.
2. Stating that he did not intervene to get security clearances when they were denied means he did.
3. Giving up his business activities means that has not and he is still running his business from the Oval Office.
4. Lowering taxes for the middle class means increasing their taxes and reducing taxes on the rich and the corporations.

Russia, Obstruction, Collusion, Porn Stars, Caravan, Infrastructure, Taxes/Audit, Inauguration Crowd Size, German Born Father, Military Pay Increase, Voter Fraud, etc. are simply the tip of the iceberg and many political and legal historians will spend decades and centuries studying this chapter in America history.

Further, as with Henry VIII, Napoleon, Alexander the Great, and had she lived beyond her early twenties Marie Antoinette, psychiatrists will study Trump especially as NPD is further researched since very little is known about what causes it or how best to treat it. This is of paramount benefit not for the narcissist, since very few seek treatment, but for the victims and if possible so people can recognize a narcissist so that they can avoid ever being a victim.

The purpose of this treatise is for the benefit of the victims. The most important group to treat is them and not the narcissist. As stated, treating narcissist is very difficult as most never seek treatment and are opposed to believe that anything is wrong with them and because methods of treatment are in their infancy. Even mitigating the effects of narcissism are improbable and so the fate of the narcissist is generally sealed early in their adult lives and therefore unfortunately many end up in jail, lonely and ostracized, or dead. Statistically this is the case because narcissists are far more likely to engage in risky or self-destructive behaviors such as drug addition, alcohol abuse, eating disorder, or high risk sexual activity. They simply do not see any risks because in their mind everything they do is great and correct.

Conversely, the victim has great potential to lead a productive, loving, and fulfilling life. Therapy and medication can certainly help but most importantly always remember that the narcissist's fate is not your fault. He will make you feel as if it is your defect that has brought him pain. You didn't work hard enough, you weren't loyal, you didn't love me enough, you were weak and didn't break the law like a told you too, you're selfish, etc. Don't feel guilty as there is nothing you can or could have done.

As we have discussed, the narcissist will condemn fault upon you and he will believe it to be true. Don't believe it. Would you believe it if they told you the sun rises in the west? No! So why do we believe some of the statements made by Trump that are just so obviously lies (crowd size, German father, number of floors at Trump Tower, etc.). Not believing his lies or deciding that you are no longer believing his lies does not mean then and now that you, the victim, are responsible for the narcissist's fate. They did not end up dead or in jail or like Napoleon in exile on Saint Helena because of you cutting off their "supply" but because they are a narcissist. If a friend who is drug user has been using your money to buy drugs and you cut him off resulting in him getting involved with loan sharks who ultimately kill is it your fault for his death? No!

In this context of the matter at hand, to the narcissist there are two groups of victims – those that leave the narcissist and those that the narcissist leaves. The simple bright news is that if you are divorced / fired by the narcissist you are in a much better and safer situation than those that leave at their own discretion. Statistically, the narcissist is less likely to "Hoover" the fired person as he will see you as someone who can no longer feed his need for "Supply." The victim who voluntarily leaves the narcissist is likely to be coerced back into a relationship with the narcissist as a result of successful hoovering.

It is this classification of victim to whom this treatise should be most beneficial. In the Trump case almost everyone on the planet is a victim of narcissism. For many it will have no consequence on their lives and notwithstanding his death or trial / incarceration once he is out of office they will likely not ever think of or hear about him again. The balance of the victims will originate from Trump supports and those who oppose him. Support or opposition encompasses both political policy and Trump's character however the severity of victimization will be derived from the character perspective.

Those inside the Trump political sphere (i.e. political appointees, right wing media personalities, administration officials, etc.) will be certainly and severely be affected, but it is the citizens, the voters and local "ground game supporters" and the door-to-door canvassing teams, whose victim experience will be devastating. It is these people who will for years to come be in incredible need of support much in the way victims of fraud, robbery, and violent crimes require ongoing emotional , psychiatric, faith based, and financial support.

Let me be extremely clear; the average Red State middle class Trump supporter is going to experience several thresholds of victimization:

1. They will feel that it is their fault. They didn't do enough. They didn't love enough and financially contribute enough and so it is their fault Trump lost the re-election, was impeached, or found criminally guilty and sitting in jail.

2. The victims will inevitably find themselves, among other things, exhausted emotionally, financially broke or struggling, and / or physically sick all of which will be caused by the ending of their relationship with their narcissist similar to the suffering experienced in divorce or from being laid off / downsized. The sense of worth and will be weakened.

3. It is then that the worst comes for the victim like a shark hunting its prey. So first let me say sorry to you because few if anyone else will say it. I'm sorry you feel tricked and misled. I'm sorry that you have lost so much even relationships or friendships with people who did not or could not see what you eventually did. I'm sorry you were called a turn coat and a traitor. I'm sorry you feel sick and sorry than no one, even psychologists and religious leaders, don't understand. I'm sorry you feel like your identity has been lost. I'm sorry your mind as been spinning and your brain appears not to be working

as it once had. I'm sorry you are feeling confused. I'm sorry for the racing heart beats and shortness of breath and all the symptoms of Post Traumatic Stress. I'm sorry your needs have been ignored and that whatever you thought you did to aid the narcissist was never enough such as; I voted for him, I went to his rallies, I stuck up for him and even to my best friends, I gave money and contributions to him -- It was just never enough and now I am left alone and scared and no one understands, not even me. I'm sorry for the hoovering that you will experience or already have.

◆ ◆ ◆

The text below comes from a YouTube video I watched after ending a personal relationship with a narcissist. I don't know what I would have done had I not seen it. Although the video describes a personal relationship with a narcissist and the inevitable hoovering as an example experience is the same in a business relationship or even if it is with a politician who is the President of the United States and someone 99.9% of the victims never met in person. The damage done to and experiences of the victim are the same and I simply couldn't do anywhere near as good a job at explaining what's ahead for many of us.

Anna Morningstar, who I will consider our YouTube expert, has many videos on the subject of NPD on the channel *Thrive After Abuse.* She describes so vividly in her work the

"Unmasking" of the narcissist, the "Grand Finale" with the narcissist, and the "Supply" for which the narcissist will "Hoover" his victims.

Note: The transcript contains minimal edits (removing or changing some of the colloquialism) of Morninstar's YouTube video, *How to Prepare Yourself for Hoovering.*

This is a video on how to prepare yourself for hoovering. If you are in a relationship or recently got out of a relationship with a narcissist it is very very common that they Hoover. Hoovering is a manipulation technique. It's named after the Hoover vacuum because it's designed to suck the victims back into the relationship. Hoovering happens generally within the first year of the ending of a narcissistic relationship. Probably the most common, within that first month or so (but it can happen decades after your relationship ends) they hoover.

So why does the narcissist Hoover? They Hoover because narcissists don't view people as people. They view us as sources of supply -- supply that somehow feeds their ego or helps them get something that they feel that they're entitled to and that they should just get for free. It could be in some form of food, clothing, sex, shelter, money, social status, public image, and those kinds of things. So if they're feeling low in any of those areas that's when they start targeting different victims and for different reasons. You've probably seen this.

Why, it doesn't really make sense? Why is he with her or why is he back with his ex? It's just whatever's convenient for them. So maybe his ex provides a house for him or is giving him money or is paying off debt, etc. and that's why they Hoover. If you're not being hoovered and I encountered this, and it sounds so crazy to say, but with my narcissist I was almost kind of bummed out that he wasn't hoovering. It was almost like that added clarification that I really didn't matter and that was so incredibly painful. In this sick way I was hoping that he would Hoover me because at least it would show that he did, in a weird roundabout way, show that he cared. But really they (narcissists) don't -- they don't care. Hoovering is not a sign that they care at all. It's a sign that they are coming back to use you. So if they're not hoovering you, it's basically that they they're not identifying you as a potential supply source at that time. However, it's very important that you prepare yourself for it because this is what gets victims sucked back into these relationships. On average victims leave a crazy relationship like this seven times before they either leave for good or they're killed so it's very important that you realize that these relationships tend to escalate the abuse which comes in many forms. There's physical, there's emotional, there's financial, there's sexual, there's psychological, and I would even say that there's spiritual and it just gets worse and worse and worse every time you go back to them.

So what can you do to prepare yourself for hoovering? Go no contact. Block them ahead of time. Block them right now on Facebook block. Block any friends and any of their family on Facebook. If possible even take your Facebook account off or develop one with a fake name for just your immediate friends. This is something that victims have a hard time with. I had a hard time with. You're probably going to want to treat this relationship like you would any other relationship where you have you know boundaries and you're assertive and you do all these things. You really can't do that with a narcissist because they are highly *manipulative. They're playing to win. They're not into open and honest communication so you really don't want to do that and you really don't even want to have open and honest communication with anybody that knows them and likes them. So if you're having friends or family asking you, "well why did you get this fake Facebook account," since you know why you are switching names just make up something because they're not going to understand what kind of relationship you went through particularly if they've never been through something like this. You could just say you know what I just needed a clean slate maybe I'll go back to my other account down the road. If people are questioning, "Why are you doing this," then don't really befriend them because the whole goal of preparing yourself for hoovering is to put a wall up around you so the narcissist can't get to you. So go no contact. Block them on Facebook. Block their phone number on your phone. Set up all their emails to go to your spam folder so you don't have that trauma of seeing that they've emailed you because that'll really ruin your day and it really I can rattle you for days if not weeks after that. I will link a video I did on the most common types of hoovering but in a nutshell it's going to be stuff like, "you know they have cancer" or "they're suicidal" or "they're an addict" or "they're truly sorry" or "they found God" or "somebody else has cancer" or maybe "they're having a heart attack" or "they found some of your stuff in one of their boxes when they moved out and they want to get it back to you" or "they need to talk to you about bills." There's going to be something that they're using to try to get you to reopen communication and the victim is probably going to feel like "well it doesn't hurt to talk to them about the phone bill right" or "oh my gosh so-and-so has cancer I need to get back to them" or "they're* suicidal, what do I do." The reality is you still do not open contact. If they're suicidal you call 911. If a mutual friend of yours has cancer you contact that mutual friend. If they have cancer sucks to be them. You do not open contact with them. It's too much of a risk because keep in mind they are out to use you as a source of supply. These people are con artists -- emotional con artists for sure and often financial con artists. So try to think of them that way. I was getting emails from my narcissist from a fake email address. This will most likely happen to you too as well. I was really mad. I didn't want to have to change my email address. I was so irritated that I had to really alter my life because of him, so hindsight being what it is I really wish I would have just not used that email address for a while. I was just being stubborn.

I caused myself a lot of unnecessary pain doing that but what I did do is I created a folder in my email for whenever he would email me and I labeled it Pet Cemetery. If you're familiar with that movie it's about a family that has a little boy and he's absolutely adorable. He gets killed and they bury him in this pet cemetery. He then comes back from the dead, but what comes back looks like the little boy and talks like the little boy but it's an evil version of the little boy. Think of a narcissistic relationship like it's a pet cemetery relationship in that once you see that mask slip you see that bad behavior, their total lack of empathy, their total lack of regard, their level of lying, and your level of deceit. It is then you realize this person might look like your ex-boyfriend or your ex-husband, they might talk like them, they might dress like them, but they are not them. The person that you loved does not exist and never existed and what's come back is evil and it will destroy you. If you let them stay in your life they will suck you dry emotionally and financially.

There is no such thing as a healthy relationship with a narcissist. It's impossible, so keep reminding yourself of that. When you start falling back into those feelings of missing them because you will and because the person that you loved was an amazing person and we would have all loved that person, right? But that person wasn't real. That person did not exist. So it's perfectly normal and understandable that you're grieving the loss of that manufactured person but separate in your mind that the person never existed, that was smoke and mirrors, that was a mask.

The reality is you have this highly destructive person now in your life that you've got to get rid of. So keep telling yourself that you don't miss him you miss who he pretended to be. Keep reminding yourself of this. I would even say write it down. I did a series of affirmations. I had a whole bunch of flashcards that I kept by my bed. I had all these different flash card so I could remind myself every single morning of the mindset that I wanted to cultivate. I did what I call my little "Buddha Board" and it was all of these sayings that I needed in my mindset that I needed to cultivate in order to stay sane because I felt like I was losing my mind. At the time I didn't know anything about narcissists or sociopaths or any of these people. I thought it was just me and I was paranoid. I couldn't sleep. I was having night terrors. All these things are normal after a narcissistic relationship. If it doesn't go away within probably about three to six months you can always see a doctor. I highly recommend that if you're having a hard time get on an antidepressant or get on the anti-anxiety medication if you're comfortable with taking them. We all need help.

The narcissist is probably going to try to contact you through other people -- possibly your children. Realize that they are incredibly charming and that they are probably telling people all kinds of stuff. They're playing the victim. They're trying to get you back. They're letting other people know that they're so in love with you that they'll do anything to make it work. They do a great job of giving lip service. They charm people with their words and a lot of times with they're their superficial actions until that mask slips and you see their awful behavior for what it really is.

You might be getting hoovered by other people. That is called a "flying monkey." That's basically where they recruit other people to attack the victim and push the victim into doing what they want. I've seen this happen with children of all ages -- even adult children. As an example, maybe it's a couple where the man is the narcissist and the woman finally wants this divorce and the guy goes and recruits the children and says, "you know I love your mother so much and she won't give us another chance." The children start pushing the mother, "Give dad another chance. He's really really sorry and I think this time he means it." How can the woman walk away now if all of a sudden the mom is the "bad guy" for wanting to get out of this craziness. Very well-intentioned good people can be turned into flying monkeys. They can assist in this hoovering process so be prepared for them to have launched some sort of smear campaign against you.

Narcissists believe they are always the victim or the hero of their own story so they are probably telling a lot of lies. The stories that they told you about all of their crazy exes are what you are now. Those people we're not crazy. They were people who ended up leaving the relationship or we're kicked out of the relationship and the narcissist had to do this whole smear campaign against them. So be prepared for the smear campaign. Be prepared for other people to really not understand what you're going through. It's really helpful to join a support group so you can bounce ideas off and get some of clarity as to how to handle the hoovering. If it does start up for you, do not let it suck you back in. It is not real -- it is not real -- it is not real -- it is not real. You're going to feel really / maybe like a cold calloused bitchy person for not responding especially if you're getting texts or emails that somebody has cancer or somebody recently died or something like that. You've really got to go into self-protection mode and you've got to think of other ways to communicate with these other people that all of a sudden have all these illnesses other than through the narcissist.

Do not let them charm you. They're going to make it seem like you're overreacting or it's no big deal or what's the harm. "What's the harm? We can text a little bit back and forth and that's okay." Don't do it. Don't open that door. Remember seven times it takes victims on average. Seven times -- think about how much time that is. That equates, in your life, how much time you're throwing away by being with these people. They don't ever change. They only get worse with age. They get worse with time. They get worse with therapy. They get worse. The more open and honest you are about issues in your relationship the worse they get because the better they get at hiding their behavior. The only strategy is to get the heck out of there. Ideally, go no contact if you can. If you can't go no contact you can use a technique called "Gray Rock." Gray rock is where you become as exciting and as reactive as a gray rock so when they start telling you things like, "I'm suicidal," "I'm an alcoholic," or "I have cancer" don't respond. Whether you have kids together or work together, don't show any emotion because they're trying to provoke you. They're trying to get some sort of *reaction out of you. That's how they know what's important to you -- by how you react, which is crazy. But because they're trying every single angle: the kids, or the parents, or the cancer, or this or that etc. As soon as you react to one of those they're going to know, "that's it. That's the crack I've been looking for," and then they're going to start tapping away on that crack until they're back into your life. So, don't give them that. Don't show any reaction. I know it's going to be so hard because you just want to probably throttle these people but they thrive off of your emotional energy -- they really really do.*

That's basically how to prepare for Hoovering, oh I forgot the biggest one. Make a list. I did this this. It's fantastic. Make a list called "For When You Miss Him" and write down bullet points of everything that's terrible that he did so when you miss him you can look at this paper, at a glance, and scan it and be like, "Oh yeah, that's why I can't have him in my life anymore. He cheated. He had children by other women that I didn't know about. He drained the bank account. He's lying to our kids. He's beating the kids. He kicked the dog. He killed the dog. He stole a car." He's done all this bad behavior so when you're having these weak moments, where you're tempted to open contact, you can read this list and it sobers you up and you're like, "That's why I can't be with them anymore."

So give any questions, comments, concerns, frustrations, ideas for videos, or you just want to say hi or you want to share part of your story, let me know. My email is going to be down below with my website and my support group and I will see you soon okay bye.

About herself, Anna Morningstar states, "I am not a therapist or expert in narcissism. I am a former psychiatric nurse turned domestic violence advocate. I have both personal and professional experiencing working with people who have been through all types of abuse, and I share both. My passion is reaching those who have experienced emotional and psychological abuse and helping them to rediscover their authentic self so that they can go forward and live their best life."

She has two support groups, one on Facebook and one on her website (both are free):

www.facebook.com/groups/HealingAfterNarcissisticAbuse

www.thriveafterabuse.com/forum

Links and information about her books can also be found at:

https://sites.google.com/site/americafirstbook

https://sites.google.com/site/arinewmanwebsite

Please remember that even though one could argue that I am an East Coast Tree Hugging Free Loving Liberal Vegan Socialist Elitist and one could argue that the Trump supporters are equally passionate on their side of the spectrum we are here for you and support you and do not judge you as you are the victim.

In this particular situation the unknown lies before us. While there have undoubtedly been many narcissists in human history who ruled over a people or a nation many of them may have been unmasked to those within their inner circle. I fear it is much worse today. The present conditions of instant mass communication and global outreach has created a perfect storm where the narcissist can have thousands and even millions of victims who he can "Hoover" effortlessly and with no risk of being exposed or legal accountability. How millions of people can recover from this will take decades and generations, incredible amounts of resources, financial and otherwise, and will have a human cost that could easily overshadow the mortality of a war. The only advice I can offer to this upcoming macro calamity is that the sooner the staunchest Trump supports in Congress and in the media realize that the Trump they knew, respected, and believed in NEVER REALLY EXISTED.

Saadia Gaon came to a conclusion that searching for proof of the unknown challenges the seeker to accept an answer even though it is something he has never seen or heard or smelled or touched etc. requiring a level of blind faith. His quest was how to accept the parallel truth of Religion and Science, whereas in this treatise it is Narcissism and how to look for it and what to do once it is found. How and when acceptance of the truth differentiates the victims of narcissism in two categories.

The first are those who have no curiosity about the subject because they do not know it even exists. Even if they claim that they would never be in a narcissistic relationship with a spouse or an employer or their political hero what defines them as victims is being in such a relationship and not knowing it due to their blind loyalty to the narcissist. The majority of Trump supporters simply do not know anything about narcissism and not until after the inevitable "Unmasking" can they begin to accept the proof and understand their victimization. This is contrasted by the second group who recognize the narcissistic relationship and exploit it such as the right wing media who care more about money than patriotism or morality or those in the administration who should recognize it and as a result of a thorough examination take any and all steps to avoid a disastrous future for the victims and the narcissist which statistically has a 100% chance of occurring.

Narcissism exists and although it needs significant more research it can explain the unfortunate present political situation. I suppose it really is "political science." There is a scientific methodology to identifying it that uses sense and intellect. There are remedies once it is found like any other illness. Those who are closest to its source (Trump) will be the last to see it and the most hurt and the most in need of our compassion and aid, notwithstanding our different views on public policy or lifestyle. We would not want to experience what they are going to and then be ridiculed or left to the side and so we should not do it to them.

Oh my gosh... 'the person that I loved did not exist!' So true. I don't miss him, I miss who I thought he was.

—ALLDOC (YOUTUBE)

UNMASKING

The Trump Responsa

The genesis for this writing like The Mueller Report UNCERTAINTINY: A Treatise on the Victims of Political Narcissism was found in my side reading during Shabbat services at my synagogue in the Holy City of Jerusalem. For the previous I referenced Sadia Gaon's most famous writing The Books of Beliefs and Opinions and this time it was The Responsa Literature (1959) by Solomon Freehof. These two books I started in the middle and would flip around to different essays much like reading a magazine.

This is where an essay about what Jewish Law says about robotics and whether a robot (even something like C3PO) could be counted in a Minyan (a quorum of 10 required for Jewish prayer i.e. if there are only nine can the robot count as the tenth). A side track to this text but interesting none the less, after several other essays and getting a feeling for the author I started at the beginning with his introduction.

I will quote from his text but he introduces his book by asking the question what is a Responsa? On any subject I always review Wikipedia not as a source but for an overall introduction to material and also to see their sources which appear to be quite researched and accurate. Then I start with the source materials to navigate my thinking. When looking for a modern definition Wikipedia states, "a modern term, used mainly for questions on the internet, is 'Ask the Rabbi'."

In my synagogue, Temple Emanu-El in Providence, Ask the Rabbi was a yearly gathering during the 3p.m. break in Yom Kippur services. As kids we would try to come up with a question to stump the Rabbis. At ten years old the classic *gotcha* question was god built the world in six days (with animals being created on the fifth day) and rested on the seventh, does that mean the dinosaurs only lived for one day? In those years the services would resume again at 4pm with the reading of the classic Jonah and the Whale story and me and my buddies would sneak into the rabbis office and eat snacks (since we were pre-bar mitzvah and not supposed to fast) while preparing for next year's question which of course was the same question.

Responsa, what is it? Like the now famous Qui Pro Quo the word Responsa is Latin (the plural Responsum) and literally means response or answer. Answers to what? For this we return to Freehoff and his introduction which begins, "If the greatness of a book may be judged by the amount of literature it has inspired, then there can be no question that the Bible is the greatest of books. The number of books which the Bible has evoked in almost every field of human thought, from the niceties of grammar to the wide sweep of philosophy, is far beyond computation. By the same test, the Talmud deserves the reverent attention of students of world literature." For simple clarification the Talmud (Jewish Law) is to the Bible like American Law passed by Congress which is based on or derived from the US Constitution. He continues about the Talmud, "In almost every great country in the world where Jews have lived, books inspired by the Talmud were continually produced and, after fourteen hundred years, are still being written.

Yes, they are still being written in what is known as post Talmudic or Rabbinic literature that Freehoff suggests exist in three basic forms. First, are the commentaries on the Talmud the most famous of which were from Rashi (11th century), the second is the codification of the law, and the third were the Responsa – the answers to questions raised aka "Ask the Rabbi." For reflection let us think of the Talmud as American Law inspired from the constitution, the commentators are the scholars of today whether it be economic, legal, religion, etc., and Responsa are simply answers to questions that are asked. These questions can be asked by anyone.

For example, in an educational forum led by Rabbi Jerry Epstein (the visionary behind the Fuchsburg Center and its Yeshiva in Jerusalem and the former Chief Executive of the United Synagogue) we were discussing the Responsa that permitted the ordination of gay rabbis in the Conservative Movement. Notwithstanding the path of the various discussions that allowed the Law Committee to issue a teshuva (in Hebrew) or a Responsa, I asked the most obvious question as to why did this issue even come up in the first place to which Rabbi Epstein replied, "because someone asked the question."

Finally, before I connect Responsa to my previous source of Saadia Gaon and finally arriving at the matter presently before all of us, for one last time I was most illuminated by Freehoff when he wrote this, "The post-talmudic or rabbinic books may well be called a hidden literature. The fact that these books were produced by a small and often persecuted people, and also that they are extremely difficult for the uninitiated to read, has confined the rabbinic literature to the circle of those who have created it. If it had been written in one of the widely known languages, or if its contents were less abstruse, it would by now have been analyzed and discussed and admired in hundreds of essays, for its contents, its keenness and its social influence, since it offers a magnificent opportunity for the study of one of the closest interrelationships between literature and life."

This passage combined with his specific thoughts on Responsa bring us to a response to the question "that is all everyone is talking about" my mother kept saying -- should Donald Trump continue as president? The first question has already been answered. The Mueller Report was commentary (like Rashi) and the first Responsa by Attorney General Bill Barr when he answered the question, yes Donald Trump should continue as President. Impeachment is the next Responsa and there will be many more. The codified law of the US is the courts' territory and finally there is the army which if necessary has always in the past ended with the passing of its' society.

THE MUELLER REPORT UNCERTAINTY – A Treatise on the victims of Political Narcissism addresses why the victims continue to support Trump in light of the circumstances before them, the painful awakening they will suffer through much like a battered woman finally opening her eyes and saying, "what was I thinking?" and the need to support them even if we vehemently oppose them politically, and narcissist's "hoovering" (i.e. stalking for lack of a better word) of them for the rest of Trump's life.

This essay intentionally is not about the law or the politics of these moments as I am not qualified to provide erudite commentary, yet I will put those in the Senate, hesitant to act pursuant to their constitutional mandate, at some ease. Senators, you are the victims of a narcissist. You are questioning the fragility before you not because you want to do that which is right and just but because you don't know how. You are the last source of "supply" to the narcissist and, like the drug dealer and addict, once the "supply" is cut off the addict leaves. The narcissist here will leave as well. Although you will be asked "what will you do, convict and remove or acquit" the victims in your states will also begin to see this unmasking of the narcissist and they will guide you and decide for you. Trust in the People. In the end, the decision will also come easy because if Trump is acquitted it will not just be like Al Pacino burying his face in cocaine, but a dictator, king, or emperor will replace the presidency and the legislature and the judiciary will be dissolved.

Using the American approach to the crisis in the Balkins in the 1990s the time has come to break up the United States of America and provide an opportunity for people to pick the type of government and society they desire. This too may also happen through its own natural evolution. For example, if Trump is not removed from office (for whatever reason such as removal or election loss) and a monarchy or Putin like autocracy is created empowered states will begin to succeed and those that do so first will be far better off than those that wait. In the event that Trump remains in power and somehow can hold the country together, please please please make him a dictator or supreme leader and not a king. Why? If he is a dictator once he passes a new dictator will take over. If he is a monarch then once he passes Don Jr. will be crowned King.

I imagine the late night hosts like Stephen Colbert, "Trump tweeted today, The election was rigged only I can save us from the deep state and so I crown... proclaim... appoint myself..."

I would say "returning to reality" to realize this is our reality. To escape it all the other two books I have been reading are General Franz Halder's War Journal and Auguste Escoffier's "A Guide to Modern Cookery" in the late 19th Century both of which provided insight and reflection while writing this.

The algorithm used to make the predictions below (while obviously proprietary) is mathematically far from scholarly, yet illuminates several factors. Without discussing the relevance or the weight of its importance in formula, suffice it to state, factors that are worthy of further material study and discussion. These factors revealed their commonality to the application of time and space in simple ways found in Halder's and Escoffier's writings.

The first prediction is what has already been discussed above; the breaking up of the United States. That process has already begun in tomorrow's vote to acquit Donald Trump. He is now The State and everything he touches dies. Bill Maher was right in pronouncing that Donald Trump would never leave. Actually before tomorrow he was saying "he will never leave."

So this first prediction is quite easy because that train has already left the station and the next one isn't far behind.

The second prediction is that Trump will commit suicide.

Referencing the previous essay, the main reason for suicide is based on the fact that there are not many 70 plus year old narcissists walking around who aren't in jail. I do not believe he will serve one day in jail but I could see a Napoleon situation (something I would argue for), or an escape ala what Michael Jackson had planned had he been found guilty. If I am wrong it means that he has become a dictator or a king.

One thing very important to remember here is that for the rest of his life he will either be a Ruler or a Prisoner. He cannot be the King of the United States because if he was the

Republic would break apart. You can't have one without the other.

It is here that I reference General Halder's War Journal and an exercise I did. I flipped 2/3 of the way and read the passage "25 Romanian high school graduates will enter the German Army as officer candidates." Two pages earlier indicated the date of this entry as 21 June 1941. Two thirds into the diary we could have expected to be much further into the war and could read Romanian teens entering the elite German officer's schools was a sign of weakness caused by depleted German candidates. We would be wrong. Halder's service ended in 1942. Halder's note is anticipating Romanian involvement in Operation Barbarossa (The German invasion of The Soviet Union) which (a) coincidently to some, (b) with knowledge of others including General Halder, and (c) in breaking the pact with Stalin, Hitler launched on 21 June 1941. Change the date, change the meaning – much in the same way that one scholar may not just be asking a question in the 17th century being answered by a scholar in the 11th century but an entire debate about the matter in question.

Finally I will end with Escofier because before you begin AMERICA FIRST A Modern Fable I am sure a snack is on the mind. Escofier is cooking decades before Downton Abbey so that is why he elaborates for the first 100 hundred pages on stocks (chicken, beef, etc.) and the elaborate and precise methods of preparation. The chefs of the day and the families' they served would partake in such feasts we could only imagine. Well we do – it's aisle eight at the grocery store – they are bouillon cubes. In almost everything we eat today the quality of the stock used to prepare it is equivalent to 1890's royalty.

What does this teach us? Sixty years it was between the French Revolution and the French Republic that still exists today. In the modern day time passes at lighting speed. I write about this in my book, *Mrs. Vanderbilt*, "Although since Biblical times the world has rotated on its axis at exactly the same speed as it does today, each generation in each century in each millennia can sense that time, for them, is moving more quickly than for their predecessors. Perhaps it is simply that through innovation and new technologies, what once took a week now takes only a day, and in one hundred years it may take only an hour, and then a minute, and eventually a second, or a fraction of second and so on."

Looking at events today requires analysis from 50 years before and 50 years ahead -- at minimum. We are simply doing what others in history have done such as the Magna Carta, King George 3, Maximilien Robespierre and the French Revolution, freeing Africa of European rule post World War 2, the race to space and the dawn of robotics – we are asking questions and the scholars are issuing responsum. I hope it is not too late.

ELECTION NIGHT

Upstairs in the White House residence President Baker and his wife, Evelyn, are seated on the couch surrounded by family, friends and young children running up and down the main foyer. An aide walks over to the President, "Sir, I just spoke with GOP headquarters and they said Ohio is still too close to call."

President Arthur Conrad Baker stares at the TV screen in disbelief, where he sees a hotel ballroom filled with people as the band plays. A banner above the podium reads "Four More Years Re-Elect Baker/Crane." A speaker comes to the microphone, "and so my friends, while the hour is late, the President still fights and so must we. We must get out there and fight for leadership and values, strength and conviction..."

At the back of the ballroom, the press, TV cameras, photographers, and reporters are updating the viewers at home, "once again on election night it seems that we are going to bed with that Florida slogan from the 2000 election, 'too close to call'."

President Baker changes the channel to an identical scene on TV with the band playing, the press corps broadcasting live from the back of the ballroom, and with another politician at the podium addressing a crowd holding signs that read "Time for Change Elect Hamilton/Clark". The TV reporters are all saying the same thing, "Here in Los Angeles at the Democratic headquarters for the Hamilton/Clark campaign, aides say that the Governor is conceding nothing and that they expect to declare victory as soon as all the ballots are counted in Ohio."

In a CNN studio veteran anchor Stanley Ropert is broadcasting. He is using a map of the United States with states colored in either red or blue. The state of Ohio is blank. "So here's where we stand as of 3am on the east coast. President Baker in red currently has 266 electoral votes, while the challenger, Democratic California Governor Conrad Hamilton in blue, has 252 electoral votes. The first candidate to receive 270 Electoral College votes wins. Therefore, Ohio with its twenty electoral votes will decide this election and once all precincts report in, we should have the result some time tomorrow morning."

At the White House reporter Rob Black updates, "With a difference of only 535 votes in Ohio separating the President and Governor Hamilton, the write-in ballots will determine who will be the next President of the United States."

Against the background of an Ohio high school cafeteria, a large number of people carefully evaluate each ballot, holding them up to the light and examining them with a magnifying glass. In the cafeteria a local reporter, "Just this morning the

Ohio Board of Elections began recounting every ballot in the state insuring that every vote was properly cast and recorded."

At the White House one month later Robert Black reports, "Day thirty of the recount brought several unexpected events. First, the Ohio Elections Board has thrown out over six hundred votes for the President placing victory in the hands of Governor Hamilton. Second, for the first time since election night, Oklahoma Governor Susan Crane spoke with reporters. As you may remember Governor Crane was asked by the GOP and President Baker to run in the Vice President's place after he stepped aside for – quote unquote - health reasons."

At the TV news studio Stanley Ropert interviews the Republican Nominee for Vice President, "Governor Crane is a hard line conservative and married to one of the GOP's largest contributors, oil tycoon Calvin Crane."

Governor Susan Crane was born November 24, 1962 the day Jack Ruby killed Lee Harvey Oswald. Her mother descends from one of the oldest families in America, who perpetuate the myth that their ancestors were on the Mayflower. She and her ailing mother are members of the Daughters of the American Revolution. Although her family was well known as Northern Republicans, she has since been anything but after attending Duke University where she met her husband Calvin. After graduation they married and returned to his home state of Oklahoma where they had twin sons Travis and Buddy. While Calvin rose through the corporate offices of Haliburton, Susan graduated from law school at the University of Oklahoma. She entered private practice but was easily seduced to run for public office. In her first election she became the Lt. Governor and years later found herself in the Governor's Mansion with a seventy-eight percent approval rating. When the incumbent Republican Vice President was dropped from the ticket she was added by President Baker.

"This is so scandalous. First we win and then the Democrats do everything, including committing election fraud, to get our votes thrown out. I think we're going to have to go back to the courts."

Stanley asks, "Isn't that exactly what you did in the 2000 election?"

Susan argues, "No, that's just left wing Hollywood liberal spin."

Outside the United States Supreme Court tens of thousands of people wave signs and cheer for their candidate. As the ruling is read, hundreds of reporters race out of the courthouse all hoping to be first with the headline. "Finally, just moments ago, after fifty-five days of recounting and going back and forth from the Ohio Supreme Court to the United States Supreme Court, the nine justices have decided in a five to four ruling that the current results of the election stand, which means that in an upset Democrat Governor Conrad Hamilton of California has defeated incumbent President Baker. On January twentieth, Governor Hamilton will be sworn in as the forty-fifth President of the United States."

One month later, somewhere in the Persian Gulf, with a new President sworn in as Commander-in-Chief, a US Navy helicopter is flying in low, off the coast heading across the desert and out over the ocean.

The chopper is filled with a platoon of forty US Navy SEALs, heavily armed and wearing night vision goggles. They are being led by 37 year-old Colonel Tanner, a tall thin man, standing directly right behind the pilot who tells him, "We're two minutes out."

Tanner turns to his lieutenant, "Two minutes."

The SEAL lieutenant yells to his men, "Two minutes. Get ready."

In Washington D.C. at the Pentagons' National Military Command Center, known as NMCC, the Operations Center is packed with computers and control panels operated by lieutenants and captains. A map of the area in the Persian Gulf is on the large screen on the wall at the front of the room. The helicopter is visible on the screen as it moves across the water.

Top generals and colonels monitor every move on the screens under the supervision of military hawk Army General Baxter and Navy Vice Admiral Fitzgerald who spent his career in command of several aircraft carriers. Forty year old Major O'Connor, the officer in charge of the NMCC, begins to sweat when Vice Chairman of the Joint Chiefs of Staff, General James (Jimmy) Hunter enters.

Hunter was born and raised in the Bayou. His grandfather was a member of the 82nd Airborne Division during World War II who parachuted into Normandy on D-Day and was later wounded during Operation Market Garden, which ended his military service with the rank of Captain and awarded both the Purple Heart and the Silver Star. After the war his family started a wholesale seafood business at which Hunter would work after school and during the summers. His father was never drafted into the Vietnam War and for years he was ashamed of not having served while many of his high school buddies never came home. The day after Hunter graduated from high school he enlisted in the Marines and maintained an excellent performance rating until being seriously wounded in the 1983 Beirut bombing of the Marine barracks. His recovery and rehabilitation took almost two years which he did in ROTC at LSU. He earned a Bachelor of Arts in Near Eastern Studies and a Master's and a Doctorate in Education. He achieved the rank of Major before being deployed to the Gulf War in 1990 during which he was promoted to Lt. Colonel. By 9/11 he was just in his second month as a Brigadier General and a decade later when American forces returned from Iraq he came home as a Lieutenant General. He was immediately nominated by President Obama and confirmed by the US Senate to the rank of Four Star General and became a Member of the Joint Chiefs of Staff to which he was eventually named its Vice Chairman. Married with two grown daughters, his life had been dedicated to the Marine Corps and he was revered as a tough warrior. He never enjoyed hunting and was quoted as saying, "I've shot enough in my life and have seen such carnage that what pleasure could I ever get to killing for enjoyment." He did, however, admit to eating meat, particularly enjoying a great Porterhouse after a day on the lake fishing.

One of O'Connor's men says, "Major, Colonel Tanner's chopper is two minutes out." Everyone in the Operations Center sees the chopper flying very low, speeding over the water and heading towards a super yacht. The chopper descends to the ocean two hundred meters from the yacht and hovers over the water.

Inside, Tanner gives his men the green light, "Blue team go - Red team go."

"Good luck," shouts the pilot as out of each side of the chopper the SEALS jump into the water and make their way toward the yacht. The pilot speaks into his radio, "This is Alpha Bird One – SEALS are in the water."

"Roger, the SEALs have been deployed," responds a radio operator from the aircraft carrier, USS Nimitz, which is in the Persian Gulf, escorted by several cruisers and destroyers.

At NMCC the door to the Operations Center opens. In walks a lieutenant with a good looking man dressed in a suit named Andrew (Guy) Beeks. He walks over to Vice Chairman Hunter who tells him, "You're late."

"Nice to see you again General - where are we?"

Major O'Connor updates him, "Colonel Tanner's team is preparing to board the yacht."

As the SEALs swim and surround the yacht, they see five terrorists guarding the main deck. Colonel Tanner issues orders to his two junior officers, "Sergeant, on my order you take those guys out. Lieutenant, you and your squad come with me."

With silencers on their weapons, the Sergeant's men kill the guards. Tanner and the Lieutenant's squad scale the side of the yacht and enter. In the main hall, a SEAL takes out two more terrorists on the second floor landing. In the main hall there are steps leading upstairs and downstairs. Following behind the Lieutenant's men, the Sergeants' squad enters the main hall. They split into two groups – half head off to secure the main floor before going downstairs, while the other SEALs proceed upstairs. Shots are heard and grenades explode as Colonel Tanner leads the Lieutenant's squad downstairs.

At the bottom of the steps they take out two more terrorists. The hallway is empty. "Clear," announces a SEAL.

There are three doors along this corridor – one on each side and one in front. They breach the two side doors with grenades. The door in front of them opens and two terrorists fire at them, hitting one of the SEALs. They fire back killing the two terrorists, "Clear."

The Sergeant's voice comes over Colonel Tanner's radio: "The main floor and second floor are secure."

The squad enters the center doors killing three more terrorists inside. The Lieutenant reports to Tanner, "All clear."

In the Operations Center at the NMCC everyone listens to the communications between the SEALs and the Nimitz while observing the monitors. The Nimitz radio operator reports, "The SEALs have secured the target. They are commencing their search of the ship now."

Hunter comments, "They better find those explosives. Otherwise the President, the Secretary, and the Chairman are going to make us all eat shit."

Aboard the yacht, the SEALs are completing their search of the room which was once the main cabin but is now piled high with an assortment of engineering equipment. Some of the containers bear the *Skull and Crossbones* poison symbol, but the SEALs quickly search through everything and eventually find what they came for – a container with the very recognizable *Ionizing Radiation* symbol on its side. The Lieutenant closely examines it and turns to Tanner, "Colonel, we're too late. The package is gone."

At NMCC, Beeks overhears the radio message. Even though clearly the youngest person in the Operations Center he does not hold back, "Well if the shit ain't there it's because it took you three days to move this team into the theatre."

Although he holds the top rank in the room, Vice Chairman Hunter is not offended by Beeks' words. Rather, he throws up his hands in frustration and turns to his subordinate, "General Baxter you want to explain to our military expert here how long it takes to move a SEAL team stationed in the mountains of Afghanistan, get them to an airport, fly them to 5th Fleet Command in Bahrain, land them on the Nimitz, brief them..."

"It would be my pleasure sir," Baxter replies just as over the radio Tanner's voice is heard.

"This is SEAL Team Commander."

"Go ahead colonel, this is the Nimitz."

"We're in the forward cabin and other than some bomb making equipment, there's nothing left here."

At NMCC, Major O'Connor announces, "Gentlemen, the satellite is coming into range right now." On the main screen on the wall a live video feed of Tanner becomes clearer, although the image is still green and grainy. His men are behind him examining the equipment.

As he points, Beeks instructs Major O'Connor, "Zoom in on that table. Are we recording?"

"Yes sir, as best we can."

"Cause I can't make out anything."

Major O'Connor responds, "As soon as the original video is back on the Nimitz we will receive a clean satellite transmission."

"Send it to my office as soon as it's in." Beeks then turns to Hunter and says, "I'm outta here. General, I suggest you secure the target until we confirm what's on that tape."

Hunter, "I agree."

"Good," Beeks continues, "Jimmy, I'll see you later at the White House." As he leaves, he acknowledges the rest of the top US military officers with a somewhat sarcastic salute, "Gentlemen."

A moment passes and General Baxter offers his opinion of Beeks, "What an asshole."

Vice Admiral Fitzgerald, "I agree."

Hunter disapproves, "Well that asshole has the ear of the President and is this nation's leading expert in nuclear warfare, proliferation, terrorism..."

Baxter, "He's still a punk."

Hunter explains, "He graduated number one from MIT with a doctorate in astrophysics and aeronautical engineering and he's fluent in five languages including Arabic."

Beeks grew up in Oahu, Hawaii as the only son of a rear admiral attached to the United States Pacific Fleet at Pearl Harbor. His mother died tragically when he was in grade school and as a way to distract himself from the loss, he became a lover of science fiction novels. Even in his teens while his friends would spend weekends in Honolulu he would stay on base and eventually developed a fascination for planes and ships and how they might one day exist like the ships and fighters he read about when he was younger. Simply, he was a genius and legendary for being the first person ever nominated to and accepted at Annapolis, West Point, and the Air Force Academy. He has never been married, and to counter his nerd brain and his top secret CIA position, he exploits his good looks as a player in the Washington D.C. nightclub scene.

"Rumor has it that he can also conduct one hell of a symphony." As Hunter finishes he instructs Major O'Connor, "Send me a copy of that tape along with Tanner's debriefing as soon as it comes in."

"Yes sir."

As Hunter leaves, Baxter orders, "Major, do it."

O'Connor speaks into his head set, "NMCC to the USS Nimitz."

"USS Nimitz, go ahead."

"USS Nimitz you have a green light on the SEAL deployment to secure the target."

"Roger, green light the SEALs." The room is dark with many computers and control panels as the Nimitz Radio operator confirms on her headset. Immediately, on the Nimitz flight deck, hundreds of SEALs, fully armed, run onto waiting Sea Knight choppers. As the SEALs board, the choppers take off into the dead of night to reinforce and secure the target.

STATE OF THE UNION

S everal days later at the White House, an SUV pulls up to the side gate and is approached by a police officer. The one driver says, "I'm here to pick up the budgets."

"ID please."

The guard takes the ID and walks into the security booth. Another guard checks underneath the vehicle with a mirror and opens the back hatch. The first guard comes back to the car and returns the ID. "You know where to go?"

"I do." The SUV drives off toward the West Wing.

Inside the Oval Office members of the National Security Council gather to brief the newly sworn-in President Conrad Hamilton. He is surrounded by Vice-Chairman of the Joint Chiefs General Jimmy Hunter, the CIA's Guy Beeks, General Baxter, Vice Admiral Fitzgerald, FBI Agent Natalie Collins who is a year or two younger than Beeks and the only woman in the room, the Secretary of Defense, the CIA Director, the Chairman of the Joint Chiefs, the White House Chief of Staff, and additional military personnel and political advisors.

Beeks, "Sir the bottom line is we don't know what they were doing there. It could be a radioactive device - it could be some bio-chemical weapon. It could also be nothing. It could be the size of a truck or fit into my briefcase."

"Clearly we need more intelligence," offers the Chief of Staff.

The Defense Secretary, "I agree."

Beeks, "The only way to get what we really need is to send in a team on the ground."

Chairman of the Joint Chiefs asks, "How soon can we get a team from Langley to the Persian Gulf?"

CIA Director, "CIA can get a team out in two hours. What about the FBI?"

Collins, "I'll send someone from my counter-terrorism task force."

CIA Director asks Collins, "You're not going?"

Collins, "I don't work for CIA anymore – and certainly not in the Middle East. When you have terrorists in Hawaii call the FBI; then I'm your girl."

The door from the outer office opens and a secretary walks up to the President, "Excuse me sir, the Secretary of Transportation has arrived."

President Hamilton tells his national security team, "Let's go do it."

Chief of Staff, "We'll reconvene via video conference in forty-eight hours. Thank you everyone."

As everyone rises and exits, Hunter walks over to the President, "I'm sorry I won't be able to join you tonight."

"Don't be ridiculous, you have more important things to do."

"I'll be back on the job in two days."

The secretary hands the President a gift wrapped package which he gives to Hunter, "General, this is for your daughter from my wife and me and wish her congratulations on her wedding."

"Thank you, Mr. President."

As they exit the West Wing the CIA Director tells Beeks, "Guy, I want you to go to the Gulf and serve as point. In fact, prepare to leave tonight."

In the parking lot Beeks notices White House staffers loading boxes into the same SUV which had recently entered the White House complex. He replies, "I was supposed to go to the State of the Union tonight. I'm bringing a date."

"Well not anymore. I need you on that plane. You're the best man we have and we need to find out what the hell is going on there before a bomb goes off in a major American city. Guy, I'll make it up to you."

Beeks notices the SUV and overhears the two White House staffers loading it.

"What is all this shit?"

"I think it's the budgets for tonight; hell of a lot of wasted paper."

Beeks asks the CIA Director, "Why the hell are they doing that today?"

In the Oval Office the President rises from behind his desk as Transportation Secretary John Wilson is escorted in, "John, I know you really didn't want to do this, but someone has to stay behind."

"It's my honor Mr. President."

"And I didn't pick you because you're the only Republican in my Cabinet."

"I didn't think so sir."

"Feel free to watch the speech here in the Oval and order whatever you want for dinner."

"Anything else I should know?" asks Secretary Wilson as the First Lady enters the Oval Office.

He notices his wife, "I'll be a moment my dear," as he reaches out his hand to her and smiles. He continues, "John we could brief you on how to be a President but I'm sure it won't come to that – after all – you're fourteenth in the line of succession."

"Come on, you don't want to be late," says the First Lady as she helps her husband put on his coat.

Secretary Wilson, "Mrs. Hamilton, what a pleasure to see you again."

She responds, "I actually saw your wife the other day at a Red Cross event."

"Yes, she did mention it."

The President and his wife leave the Oval Office as Wilson sits on the couch and pulls out his cellphone. The President's secretary turns on CNN whose camera is positioned directly at the exterior of the US Capitol.

On the other side of Pennsylvania Avenue the SUV from the White House has parked at the Capitol building. One officer of the Capitol Police is barely paying attention as the same two drivers carry the boxes inside.

Ten miles east of Washington D.C. at Andrews Air Force, Beeks exits a Lincoln Town car, runs across the tarmac, and boards an Air Force Gulfstream. "Let's get out of here."

The President and his wife exit their limousine surrounded by Secret Service agents and enter the Capitol.

On a commercial 737 airplane Hunter is dressed in civilian clothes sitting in first class. He reads a novel as a flight attendant hands him a glass of champagne. He looks up and says, "Thank you." As his eyes move back to his book he glimpses on his small video screen the inside of the US Capitol as the State of the Union is about to begin.

The room is filled with Senators and Representatives. Mrs. Hamilton is in the balcony. In the front rows are the Supreme Court Justices in their traditional black robes, the highest ranking generals and admirals, and Cabinet members.

The doors in the back of the chamber open. The Crier walks through, stops, and shouts, "Here Ye, Here Ye, Mr. Speaker, the President of the United States." Everyone applauds as the President enters and begins shaking hands.

Across town FBI counter terrorism expert Natalie Collins opens the door to her apartment and drops her bag on the floor. She walks into her bedroom and turns on her TV set. She falls onto her bed with her clothes on. On the TV, the President is about to deliver the State of the Union address – making his way to the podium. She falls asleep. "And so my fellow Americans, I am pleased to announce tonight that the era of big government is over, and a period of productive government is beginning. Here tonight we are all united, facing a bright future and assuring prosperity and freedom for all..."

"I think this is the same speech as his Inauguration."

"This one's worse," responds Kelly, the CNN Producer, as laughter fills the control room. She is in charge of the broadcast and oversees a team of technicians, assistant directors and co-producers. The President appears on all the screens. The phone rings. She picks it up, "This is Kelly. Oh hi sweetie. Did you finish your homework? Mommy will be home by midnight... Ok goodnight. Put daddy on the phone. Hi...Hello. Hello?"

All the TV monitors have suddenly gone black and the Director asks, "What the hell? Did we just go black? Did we just lose power?"

Kelly moves the phone away from her head, "What happened?"

"We must have lost power."

She asks, "Are we still broadcasting?"

"No," responds one of the Assistant Directors.

The Director, "Are you sure?"

"And neither is anyone else," responds one of the co-producers as everyone looks up and sees that all the monitors indicate the other networks broadcasting the speech have also gone black.

The TV in the Oval Office is also not broadcasting anymore. Secretary Wilson changes the channel hoping that will help but all the channels are black and an announcement can be heard, "We are temporarily experiencing technical difficulties."

The phone rings again. A technician answers, "Hello." Then another ring and another - then every phone. Kelly looks around and her entire team is scrambling to figure out what's happening.

Somebody shouts, "The feed must have been cut."

"Well, fix it," responds the Director.

One of the co-producers hands Kelly a phone, "Kelly, it's Rob at the White House."

"Not now."

Screaming to get Kelly's attention, "He says there's been an explosion!"

The control room goes silent as everyone freezes in disbelief. Kelly, demands, "I want playback in three, two, one, playback."

The TV monitor rewinds for three seconds and then plays the President delivering the State of the Union, "This nation shall not give into Terro..."

The screen goes black.

The door bursts open and a half dozen secret service agents enter the Oval Office. They run directly to Wilson, "Sir, you must come with us immediately."

In the control room Kelly picks up the phone. "Rob, what's going on at the White House?" She tells her team, "Get a camera on him now." Rob is standing in the shot holding his cell phone with Kelly on the other end. Secret service agents and White House police officers are running around, some with barking dogs, as the White House press corps goes live one by one on their networks. Over Rob's shoulder past the front façade of the White House an orange glow illuminates the Washington D.C. sky line.

At the security gate house Rob sees chaos, as West Wing staffers, plain clothed and uniformed Secret Service agents have guns drawn and White House police officers watch the security monitors. Some are on the phone. A phone rings and an officer answers it, "White House security gate 4."

The officer turns around and hands the phone to a Secret Service agent. Other agents run out of the West Wing. Wilson is rushed through the hallway as the agents shout: "Let's go, let's go. Move it. Out of the way. Clear the hall." Everyone moves to the side while others are pushed out of the way and knocked to the ground.

Outside, a motorcade of black SUVs wait by the entrance flashing red and blue lights. Secret Service agents with guns drawn surround the vehicles. The West Wing entrance doors swing open as Wilson and the agents get him into the vehicle. The agents hop on the sides of the SUVs and they speed off. Other Secret Service SUVs race in and out of the grounds as a White House police officer approaches the press corps followed by Secret Service agents.

Rob, on the phone, "Kelly, all I know is – hold on."

The police officer instructs everyone, "We are evacuating the White House. Everyone needs to leave now. We are in a code red."

Rob asks Kelly, "Did you hear that?"

"Yup," Kelly has two phones up to her ears. "Get out of there but stay on the line."

In the CNN control room one of the technicians announces, "The AP is reporting an explosion at the Capitol building."

"Oh my God," the Director is in shock.

Kelly yells, "Someone find Stanley in Atlanta and get him in the chair now."

The Assistant Director picks up the phone, "Hi this is control B we need Stanley Ropert in the chair right now. There's been an explosion at the State of the Union."

As people run in and out of the control room Kelly asks the Assistant Director, "How long?"

"They said two minutes. He's in the bathroom. Someone went to get him."

Kelly tells her Director, "As soon as you have an aerial shot and Stanley, go live with the Breaking News logo." Still with two phones to her ears she orders the Assistant Director, "Call Euro Satellite now. We better be first in Europe with this one."

"Look," responds the Assistant Director. They both see that one of the monitors shows multiple F-15 Strike Eagles taking off from the runway at Andrews Airforce Base.

A thousand miles away in Oklahoma, Governor Susan Crane and her husband Calvin Crane watch TV. Their screen is black. Susan, "Change the channel," as Calvin flips through the channels but they are all black. Her phone rings. Susan picks it up, "Hello." The TV picture comes back on -

BREAKING NEWS and says, "We interrupt this program for a special report."

"Good evening. Stanley Ropert reporting from CNN headquarters in Atlanta. Approximately five minutes ago, a massive explosion occurred at the Capitol building during the President's State of the Union Address."

In the control room Kelly and her team watch Stanley on the TV monitor. The Assistant Director announces, "Rob is ready."

Stanley on TV, "The Associated Press is reporting that the Capitol is completely engulfed in flames. People have been seen running out with severe burns and in some cases actually on fire."

Kelly, speaking into Stanley's earpiece, "Go to Rob."

Stanley on TV, "Capitol police have evacuated the area. Now we are going live to White House chief correspondent Rob Black who is standing on Pennsylvania Avenue just outside the gates of the White House. Rob what can you tell us?"

Standing on Pennsylvania Avenue on TV, "Within the last ten minutes there has been what appears to be a major explosion at the U.S. Capitol. The building is completely on fire. As you can see from these aerial shots, the Capitol has been virtually – totally destroyed, but we don't yet know what caused the explosion. Of course since 9/11, everyone's initial reaction is that we are probably looking at an act of terrorism, but that is just peculation at this point. The White House staff has confirmed that the President and the Vice

President were both in the Capitol building at the time of the explosion."

CNN shows pictures of massive flames shooting out from where the Capitol building's giant dome once was. It has been completely destroyed. People can be seen fleeing the area as police, fire and EMS personnel help the victims in make-shift triage locations. Everyone around the country and throughout the world is glued to their TV screens – in every home and bar, in every major city thousands stand shocked looking at jumbotrons. The images appear on every airplane, each monitor in each seat and on every channel including on a 737 somewhere in the sky over Kentucky where Hunter has fallen asleep still holding his book. A flight attendant pokes him in the arm, "Mr. Hunter."

No response. She tries again, "Mr. Hunter."

"Yeah."

"The captain has asked me to give you this message."

While he's reading it an announcement is made from the flight deck, "Ladies and Gentlemen this is your captain speaking. I understand many of you have seen the reports on your video screens." Hunter and the flight attendant make their way to the flight deck as the captain continues, "This is obviously a national emergency and so Air Traffic Control has ordered a nationwide ground stop. We have been instructed to return to Dulles." Hunter knocks on the cockpit door.

The door opens and Beeks walks into the Gulfstream cockpit. The pilot breaks the news to him, "Mr. Beeks we've been ordered by the Pentagon to turn around. There's been an explosion at the U.S. Capitol building."

Beeks, "What?"

"You can turn on the TV in the cabin."

Beeks walks back into the cabin. He turns on CNN and sees Rob continuing his report from Pennsylvania Avenue, "We can also confirm at this time that almost every member of Congress and all nine members of the Supreme Court were in the building at the time of the explosion."

Natalie Collins is asleep on a couch. Her beeper goes off. Her phone rings. Her cell phone rings. There is a knock at the door – banging on the door. She eventually wakes up and picks up her cell phone. She yells to the door, "Hold on." She answers her phone, "Hello." With more banging at the door, she speaks into the phone, "Hold on," and then yells towards the door, "One second!" Wearing her clothes she wore the day before, she walks to the door looking at her beeper. She looks at the clock. It reads "9:50". "Who is it?"

Collins grew up in Fargo, North Dakota in a family of practicing Lutherans who emigrated from Scandinavia. Although socially conservative, she accepted a full academic scholarship to Smith College, a prestigious liberal leaning all women's university in the Massachusetts Berkshire Mountains. She went on to earn a Doctorate in International Relations from George Washington University and was working in the State Department when she was recruited into a CIA training program. As threats of ISIS sympathizers materialized in the United States she was transferred to FBI

Headquarters. She leads a very private life, never wears anything but pantsuits and was briefly engaged to a lawyer whom she left after discovering that he was cheating on her.

At Dulles airport the 737 has pulls up to a gate, and the plane door opens from which Hunter exits. Inside the terminal, several military personnel calmly stand just outside the jet-way waiting for Hunter. The gate area is jammed-packed with nervous, scarred, and crying passengers. When Hunter approaches them they salute, "General, this way sir." They exit the terminal by walking down some steps and onto the tarmac and enter an SUV in which small screens broadcast the news coverage.

On CNN Stanley looks visibly shaken. He clears his throat and removes his glasses, "With extreme sorrow, we must inform our viewers that the White House and the Secret Service have confirmed that both President Hamilton and Vice President Clark have been killed this evening." In the Gulfstream, Beeks watches as the plane lands at Andrews Air Force Base. Stanley continues, "We can also report that the leadership of the House and the Senate are among those who have lost their lives tonight. Let us offer our prayers to their families and all Americans." He pauses, "All right let's go back to Rob Black at the White House."

It's not long before Hunter enters the NMCC Operations Center at the Pentagon. Major O'Connor is in charge. The room is bustling with military officers running all about and shouting into the phones and at each other.

O'Connor's greeting, "General Hunter."

"What's the status?"

"All airspace over Washington has been cleared. General Baxter scrambled the F-15's out of Andrews. They're patrolling over DC and he is holding on the line from NORAD."

Hunter asks, "Where are the Chairman and the Secretary of Defense?"

O'Connor answers, "The Chairman was killed along with the entire Cabinet."

"Who's in charge?"

"Secretary Wilson was evacuated from the White House and is on route to Evac Station C at Camp David."

"No, who's in charge of military command?"

"You are sir."

General Baxter appears on the monitor on the wall.

Hunter acknowledges him, "General Baxter, take us to DEFCON 2 and put the Nimitz on ready alert."

Baxter replies, "Yes Sir."

"Also let's land all aircraft, commercial and private, in the U.S. until we rule out a coordinated plane attack."

"It's already done."

At Camp David President Wilson, his wife, and a judge dressed in a black robe stand together as Wilson takes the oath of office. White House staff members and secret service agents with guns drawn witness the oath as a White House photographer takes pictures.

"...and will to the best of my ability preserve, protect and defend the Constitution of the United States."

The Judge, "Congratulations, Mr. President." The new first lady hugs her husband with tears running down her cheeks.

Within minutes of taking the oath of office, President Wilson is on video conference from the Camp David Situation Room surrounded by aides and military officers. The only one who stands out is carrying the "football," the briefcase containing the nuclear codes and protocols . At the NMCC Operations Center Major O'Connor tells Hunter, "President Wilson is on video conference from Camp David."

Hunter sees the new Commander-in-Chief, "Mr. President."

"General Hunter, I'm appointing you acting Chairman of the Joint Chiefs."

"Proud to serve, Sir - particularly at this tragic time."

President Wilson's first order, "Immediately secure our borders, close all airports and ports, organize a task force to investigate this, and you and your team be at the White House tomorrow morning – 6am."

"Sir, you don't want to meet now?"

"General, I have a nation to comfort and a government to form tonight."

Beeks and Collins walk in together as President Wilson reiterates, "You're in charge. Assemble your team. Keep us updated and we'll talk in the morning."

On the main screen at the Operations Center everyone goes silent as CNN shows footage of President Wilson being sworn in. Narrating the coverage, Stanley announces, "This is just coming in. In this footage just released by the White House Communications Office, you can see former Secretary of Transportation John Wilson being sworn in as the forty-fifth President of the United States."

The broadcast continues with Stanley interviewing Susan Crane. "Governor Crane, thanks for joining us from Oklahoma at this difficult time. Now that President Wilson has been sworn in, what's the next step?"

"Thank you Stanley. First, I'd like to extend my condolences to the families of those who perished in this terrible event."

"I'm sure everyone around the world expresses the same thoughts and prayers."

Governor Crane continues, "With respect to the government, both the Democrat Governors' Caucus and the Republican Governors' Caucus will be convening via teleconference overnight to appoint an interim House and Senate. I'm sure the President will nominate cabinet positions and Supreme Court jurists for Senate confirmation within the next several days."

Stanley asks, "What about figuring out who's responsible? How will we proceed with an investigation to determine who's behind this attack?"

"I'm sure the new President will meet with his generals and all assets of the United States will be used to hunt down and kill those responsible."

"To kill them?"

"We must redouble our efforts in fighting groups like ISIS, Boko Haram, and Al Qaeda. We must wipe radical Islamic fighters off the face of the earth."

"Governor, I just hope that whoever is responsible for this -- we take action against them and not get into another sink hole like Iraq."

"What does that mean?"

"The U.S. invaded Iraq, even though it was Al Qaeda who attacked us on 9/11, and then we couldn't get out of there. And when we finally did, the Middle East was set ablaze."

"Again, I will say we must defeat radical Islam."

THE NEXT DAY

Hailing from the State of Texas, John Wilson lived the life of a traditional Republican politician. The son of a high school teacher and a librarian he graduated from the University of Texas and attended the Yale Law School where he made Law Review. After returning to Texas, he clerked for the United States Court of Appeals for the Fifth Circuit. He served as a federal prosecutor with one of the highest conviction rates and became well known for prosecuting Timothy McVeigh in 1995. He was elected Texas Attorney General and eight years later he was elected Governor. Although greatly admired for his moral values and religious lifestyle within the national Republican Party, he failed to win his party's nomination in their last contested presidential primary.

The following morning at the White House, the sun is shining brightly, without a cloud in the sky. Pennsylvania Avenue is blocked off by the police and Secret Service. Four black SUVs drive past the White House, pass through a security gate, and stop in front of the West Wing. Hunter, Vice Admiral Fitzgerald, Beeks, Collins, and several other military officers exit the SUVs and proceed to their meeting in the Oval Office.

While they walk, Beeks argues with Collins, "The Middle East desk at Langley is convinced we're talking about Islamic fundamentalists. Why do you insist it's not?"

She responds, "It's like any other crime. Means – opportunity – motive. What's the motive?

"The motive is to get us out of the Middle East so they can create a caliphate."

"And you do that by taking out the US government and putting a Republican in the White House?"

"Be realistic. If they didn't do it, then who the hell did?"

"Listen, on 9/11 we lost three thousand Americans and in retaliation invaded two countries. If they want us out of the Middle East to create a caliphate, they don't do something that even they know will lead to an all-out war in the Arab World. They're crazy, not stupid. It doesn't make any sense."

Just outside the Oval Office, the Secret Service maintains the highest level of vigilance as they stand at their posts. As they enter, Beeks whispers to Collins, "If you tell the President it wasn't Islamic terrorists, he's going to think you're crazy."

As day breaks in Oklahoma, Susan is speaking on the phone. Calvin is also on the phone but sitting at a desk. A black woman dressed in an outdated black and white maid's uniform enters the room and serves coffee.

Susan is in a political mindset, "Well I assume The President will appoint a cabinet and jurists that are consistent with our conservative Republican philosophy."

Calvin whispers to her, "You should be the V.P."

In the Oval Office, the President, Hunter, Vice Admiral Fitzgerald, Beeks, Collins, some military officers and White House staffers are meeting.

Beeks suggests, "Well sir, regarding method, we're sure it was a bomb and not a missile or a plane. In terms of who did this, at this point we have three possibilities. I think we were attacked by terrorists, Natalie believes..."

"I can speak for myself. I believe the odds of foreign terrorists pulling off something like this is one in a million. I think we're more likely looking at some sort of domestic plot."

The President asks, "What's the third possibility?"

Collins answers him, "It was an attack to change the government, not to destroy it -- essentially a coup d'état."

Hunter asks, "What about a foreign government?"

Beeks answers, "State doesn't believe that's what we're looking at. But we'll know more once Natalie and I get down to the Capitol and meet with FBI forensics."

The disagreement continues in the hall just outside the Oval Office with Hunter telling Beeks and Collins, "If this was a coup, you two will have to look at everybody."

Beeks, "At least those that are still alive."

Hunter is concerned, "Well, find out quickly before we end up at war with the wrong people. If the President believes

Islamic fundamentalists are behind this, he'll bomb the shit out of the Middle East. Most important, find out if it's over, or if more attacks are coming."

The investigation begins at the FBI forensics lab which looks like all the forensics labs on TV put together. Beeks and Collins are being briefed by the Chief forensics scientist, a very senior man both in years at the agency and in life. The Chief asks, "Do you want to hear about the bomb?"

"Save it. It exploded and everyone died." Beeks is still agitated from listening to Collins' ridiculous theories and annoyed with Hunter for entertaining them.

"Andrew," Collins realizes that the Chief was just insulted. "Sorry Chief, we haven't slept in days."

The Chief reports, "Your explosive was the equivalent of two five thousand pound bunker busters. It could have sunk an aircraft carrier. The good news is that it wasn't released from a plane. It was already in the Capitol when was it detonated. We know this because when a bunker buster is stationary when it detonates, it blows up and out far more that if you were to fire it from a plane or a ship. Plus, any plane able to carry such weapons would have been picked up on radar."

Collins asks, "So it was definitely in the building before it exploded?"

Beeks adds, "How the hell did it get there?"

After being insulted the Chief is frustrated with Beeks, "that's your job to figure out." He returns to his work station that is covered with his lunch and turns on CNN.

Rob White is reporting from the White House lawn over historical footage. "Good evening. In the latest report from the White House, we have learned that President Wilson has nominated four conservative jurists and five others who are considered moderate to liberal. President Wilson said that he wanted to maintain the same balance on the court that existed before the attack on the Capitol. The White House also said today that the Vice Presidential nominee will be announced tomorrow and of course will require confirmation by the Senate. To put this into historical perspective, the last time something like this happened was in 1973, when Speaker of the House Gerald Ford was appointed VP by then President Richard Nixon, following Vice President Spiro Agnew's resignation after he pleaded no contest to tax evasion and money laundering. As you may remember, Ford became President in 1974 after Nixon resigned due to the Watergate scandal."

In Oklahoma, Susan and Calvin Crane are also watching CNN. Rob continues, "Some of our sources are saying that as part of the healing process for the nation, the President will probably nominate a Democrat, perhaps a current governor or even a former Secretary of State."

Calvin suggests, "Susan, you need to get on a plane and meet with Wilson tomorrow. You should be appointed. You've earned it."

"He'll never do it."

"Well, you can be frank with him. Tell him he either appoints you or he will have a very short term. We'll put our energies someplace else."

In the Oval Office twenty-four hours later, the President and Susan sit alone opposite each other. Susan tries to make her case, "I understand that for the sake of the country, you want to maintain the status quo. However, as a Republican I'm sure you would agree that a strong Republican executive branch is also in our nation's best interest."

"I appreciate your thoughts. However, I have decided to go with the Democratic governor from Florida."

"You're going with Martinez? He's as liberal as they come. He's a Mexican. He would make every illegal a citizen tomorrow."

"I understand you are disappointed. Maybe you should think about an ambassadorship or even a cabinet post, once things settle down."

"Don't be a fool. If you don't make me Vice President, you know I can destroy you."

The President stands up, smiles and extends his hand. Susan stands, but doesn't shake his hand.

"Good day Susan. I think you're looking to bite off more than you can chew. Don't go searching for trouble. Right now this nation needs to stand together."

Susan storms out.

A few blocks from 1600 Pennsylvania Avenue at FBI Headquarters Collins and Beeks are reviewing their evidence.

Beeks ponders to himself, "So how did the bomb get into the Capital?"

"Someone on the inside you think?"

"Must be."

She suggests, "So let's assume the explosives were in the containers on that SUV you saw since Capitol security records indicate that the only truck allowed access to the building that evening was the truck carrying the budgets."

He agrees, "That's how they must have done it. Did you put out an APB on that truck?"

"Chances are it is long gone, but if it's still here, we'll find it."

Beeks hopes, "Maybe we'll get lucky. Don't forget the first group to bomb the World Trade Center wanted a refund on the deposit for the truck they used to detonate the bomb and that's how we caught them."

An FBI agent walks in and informs them, "State Police got a tip from a clerk at a motel. We think we've got the truck and we have the driver in custody."

In an FBI interrogation room the prisoner is sitting in a chair in the middle of the room and there is no other furniture. Beeks and Collins walk in.

In Arabic, Beeks begins, "So you're the one that is going to be charged with the murder of the President of the United States."

The prisoner looks down.

Beeks continues in Arabic, "If you think you are a hero for your Muslim brothers you are kidding yourself. No one knows you exist, and you will be held by our government indefinitely. And while you are waiting we will destroy your family."

The prisoner answers him in English, "You don't know what you're talking about."

Collins asks, "What do you mean?"

He says nothing.

Beeks, "So you do speak English."

The prisoner, "I say nothing."

Beeks goes back to Arabic, "I'll be direct, you either answer us truthfully or I will remove a piece of your body. You know the rumors about American soldiers torturing Muslims?"

Collins clears her throat at Beeks. Beeks is surprised that she understands Arabic. The prisoner looks scared.

Beeks continues, "They're all true. So, let's start with a simple question. How did you get access to the Capitol and who is your contact in the White House?"

The prisoner says nothing.

As Beeks opens the door, two CIA agents walk in with two military officers and he orders them, "Strip him."

As they do Beeks asks Collins, "So what do you think?"

"Food denial and sleep deprivation?"

He responds, "We don't have time."

She concurs, "I agree. What about truth serum?"

"The Israelis don't find it very effective and it takes at least a week."

She offers a suggestion, "I hate to say it, but since we have ongoing presidential authority, go for it. I'd chop off a finger first, since he'll probably think you're bluffing, and after that tell him you'll chop off his jewels."

Beeks brags, "It won't be my first circumcision."

Collins doesn't want to be there when he does it, "Just hurry it up. I'm going for coffee." She exits the interrogation room and closes the door.

While Beeks begins his interrogation in D.C., in Oklahoma Susan and Calvin Crane are having dinner in their dining room. "Calvin, when I threatened him he threatened me back."

"So let's go to the next level."

Susan asks, "What do you mean?"

"Convene the Republican Governors' Caucus and secede. I'll call my guys and we'll guarantee the support of the governors. With their support you'll control half the US National Guard."

She's concerned, "We'll have nothing more than a militia."

Calvin expresses his wisdom, "We'll have power and then we'll cut a deal. It's not like there's any court we can go to for a remedy. Besides, moderates in the Blue States will align with us."

Susan prays, "Let's hope so."

While the politicians politic, the investigators investigate. At FBI headquarters, Collins is asleep at her desk when Beeks walks in holding coffee. The clock reads 6am; CNN is on. He hands her the coffee, "I stopped at Starbucks."

She asks, "How late were you up with him?"

"It took less than an hour."

"Is he dead? Don't tell me that. I'm with the FBI now – I don't want to know. Just tell me, did you get what we needed?"

Beeks answers, "He was hired by a law firm downtown and yes he is alive – and yes he has all his fingers as well as his jewels."

On CNN in Collins' office, Stanley Ropert is in the anchor chair with BREAKING NEWS. "We go live right now to Chief White House correspondent, Rob Black."

"Thank you Stanley. It appears the Constitution and our greater American union may be in grave jeopardy this morning. The Associated Press is reporting that Oklahoma Governor and former Vice Presidential candidate Susan Crane has announced the call-up of the Oklahoma Nation Guard. Governors of several states have followed suit. As of now they include Kansas, Alabama, Mississippi, Georgia, and Texas."

Upon hearing this Beeks looks at Collins, "The country is collapsing. We've got to track down that law firm."

Collins jumps up, "Let's go."

In Oklahoma at the Crane Ranch, Calvin sits in his worn out leather chair. He's smoking a cigar and holding a scotch. There are two other gentlemen with him. One is noted Washington D.C. attorney Skip Garrison, and the other is one of the wealthiest oil drillers and bankers in America, the obese and infamous Howard Mellon from Pittsburgh.

Calvin says, "I'm sending my boy, Buddy, to San Diego. General Baxter is moving to within one hundred miles of the naval port. He believes he can seize the ships within twenty-four hours."

Skip is confidant, "General Baxter will be able to see this through. He's a patriot."

Calvin asks, "How far do you want to take this?"

Mellon answers, "Well the President and the Senate will either agree to shared power or we'll control all the Red States."

Skip is confidant, "Howard, don't worry. We've been doing this since the 1950s. Do you really think that elections determine our leaders? No, we do. We decide who gets the money. We've been orchestrating elections forever and the couple of hundred votes the Democrats stole in Ohio still doesn't make this a democracy. You're still running things."

Mellon, "Just make sure we don't have another Watergate. I'm not going through what my father dealt with."

Skip walks over to Mellon and looks him in the face, "Your father was my father's client. My name's on the firm – we'll take care of everything.

Skip and Mellon shake hands before Skip leaves the room. Once he's gone, Calvin tells Mellon, "Don't worry, there's no Howard Hunt Jr. running our operation."

In Washington D.C. at the law firm of GARRISON, ROPES, & WELSH LLP, Collins and Beeks approach the reception desk along with a team of federal agents.

"Can I help you?" asks the receptionist.

"I'm Natalie Collins with the FBI and we'd like to see Skip Garrison."

"He's not in."

Collins presents a document, "This is our search warrant. Please call a senior accounting officer. We want to speak with them as well."

At the White House, President Wilson has called Hunter into the Oval Office for an emergency meeting. The President breaks the bad news, "Baxter has left NORAD. He's now working for Susan Crane."

Hunter informs the President, "We've secured all of our ballistic nuclear missiles. Baxter is two days away from taking the San Diego naval port. We need to move the fleet into the Pacific, now."

"Hunter get out there immediately. Oversee it and prepare for a counter attack."

At the law firm of GARRISON, ROPES, & WELSH LLP Collins, Beeks, and the federal agents are finally making progress after reviewing every file in Skip Garrison's office. Several agents interview the secretaries while others examine computers. One announces, "We found something."

Collins and Beeks approach the agent reviewing the computer and he shows them a file, "Here it is - a purchase order for your truck."

Collins asks the secretary, "Where is Skip Garrison?"

"He's in the Midwest."

Beeks asks the secretary, "Can you pull up a list of his contacts?"

"That would fall under attorney client privilege."

Collins interjects, "Thanks to the Patriot Act there is no privilege. Besides we're not interested in his clients, we're investigating him for murder and treason."

Beeks, "Natalie, look at this."

Beeks, Collins and the agent are looking at the computer. On the screen, a list of Garrison's contacts appears. They notice that Clarence Wilson is on the list. Beeks thinks out loud, "What's the connection between Garrison and Wilson?"

Collins asks the secretary, "How well does Mr. Garrison know President Wilson?"

"I believe they went to Yale together."

At the San Diego Air Base at Miramar, Hunter and other military officers exit a Learjet and approach the waiting SUVs. Admiral Fitzgerald greets Hunter.

Hunter quickly asks for a status report.

"We've moved the Ronald Reagan, the Stennis, and the brand new CVN-77 to about 150 miles off the coasts of San Diego and Los Angeles. Their accompanying battle groups are being deployed now."

"What about aircraft?"

"Two squadrons, approximately one hundred fighter jets, mainly from bases in Nevada and the California desert, have defected to the other side. All other aircraft have been redeployed to Blue States, primarily in the northeast and the northwest. We also have aircraft patrolling above all major US cities."

Hunter asks, "Where's Baxter?"

Fitzgerald continues, "He's got Governor Crane's troops fifteen miles from the port. He has a division of ten thousand soldiers, about 200 tanks, and a similar number of armored and transport vehicles all waiting for the go order. No movement yet though."

Not far off in the California desert, Calvin and Susan's son, Buddy Crane, exits one of the landing helicopters and is greeted by General Baxter.

He asks Baxter, "When are you deploying?"

Our forward deployed troops are two miles to the east of San Diego. They should enter the city within the hour."

While an American Civil War appears unavoidable on the west coast, in Washington D.C. late into the night Collins and Beeks examine their case files in Collins' FBI office.

Beeks, "So our theory now is that this Garrison lawyer hired the terrorists."

Collins, "Yeah, but for who? Who was he working for and what was his motive?"

He suggests, "Let's assume that Garrison and Wilson were in on this together. Was their motive to take over the office of the President of the United States?"

"If you're right, how could Wilson have known that he was to be the cabinet secretary asked to stay behind during the State of the Union?"

"And how could we ever prove it?"

Collins expresses concern, "If we're right and the White House finds out what we're on to, you know they'll kill us."

"How would they ever find out?"

"What about Hunter? We'll need to tell him what we're thinking."

Beeks states, "He can be trusted."

"Would you risk your life on it?"

"I would."

Collins suggests, "There is another possibility we should consider. Perhaps Wilson was framed."

RED, WHITE, & BLUE

In San Diego, the sun sets over the Pacific Ocean. On the streets, Baxter's forces enter the downtown area and advance toward the port. M2A3 Bradleys, M1 Abrams tanks, and Humvees slowly drive through the city with soldiers following behind before splitting off down the side streets advancing on the port.

In the CNN studio, Stanley Ropert anchors, "We interrupt this program for breaking news out of San Diego." News helicopters cover the attack like it was an LA police chase. On the empty streets of San Diego, police officers fire at Baxter's soldiers. His tanks return fire, destroying most of the police cars. Stanley continues, "As you can see from these pictures, military forces backing the so-called "Red State" break-away government led by Governor Susan Crane have entered the downtown area of San Diego. Tanks are rolling through the city as thousands of soldiers advance toward the naval port. White House correspondent Rob White is joining us live, from San Diego. Rob, what can you report?"

The San Diego border with Mexico is closed. Cars are backed up for miles. Baxter's men advance under fire as the soldiers under Hunter's command defend their positions. Rob reports, "Thanks Stanley. It appears that soldiers loyal to the break-away Red State government, which now calls itself the Confederated States, have taken military control of downtown San Diego. This exclusive aerial footage shows that for the first time in one hundred and fifty years, two groups of American soldiers are battling each other."

The Confederated States soldiers have captured the port but failed to secure any ships because Hunter was able to reposition the Union navy miles out to sea. The battle is over – General Baxter and Governor Crane's Confederated Army have won the first battle.

On an Air Force Learjet, Hunter is speaking on the phone while Fitzgerald, sitting across from him, is also on the phone. Fitzgerald hangs up and tells Hunter the bad news, "We lost San Diego."

Hunter responds, "Order them to retreat to Orange County and protect the nuclear reactor at San Onofre."

An aide approaches them, "NMCC on line three."

Hunter picks up the phone and hears a report, "Chairman Hunter, General Baxter has moved an armored infantry division to within one hundred miles of Las Vegas. It's on TV right now."

Hunter tells his aide, "Turn on the TV." The aide does.

The broadcast shows everyone in the Las Vegas casinos watching the news on every TV channel. On CNN Rob reports, "What is now being called the Confederate Army is, according to the Associated Press, advancing towards Las Vegas and could enter the city sometime tonight." As soon as the gamblers hear his words, everyone in the casinos runs for the exits in a mad rush trampling over each other.

In the Nevada desert just outside Las Vegas, General Baxter exits his Humvee. A Colonel approaches him, "We'll rest here for two hours and take the city in the morning."

"Colonel, just make sure the airport is closed."

The Colonel replies, "Planes are taking off as quickly as the airlines can turn them around. I think we're better off letting people evacuate. People are fleeing north and east of the city in cars. Let's let them leave. Holding them hostage will just complicate matters."

"I don't care about hostages."

A soldier approaches him, "Phone call for you, General."

"Baxter here."

"General, it's Calvin. I'm sitting here with the guys. We want to know how long before we can take Washington DC."

Baxter responds, "The day after tomorrow."

The next morning, Collins is sitting in her FBI office staring at her computer when Beeks walks in.

She says. "Guess what I found on Yale's website?"

He offers her, "Coffee?"

"Yeah. Thanks."

He looks at her computer, "So what did you find?"

"Guess who else went to Yale with Garrison?"

Jokingly, "Tom Brady?"

"Who? How about Calvin Crane."

"Susan Crane's husband?"

Collins explains, "Her husband is also a steel and oil tycoon. All three were in the same fraternity."

"We need to brief Hunter."

As the sun rises over the western desert in San Diego the next morning, Confederate soldiers enter a government Detention Center for illegal aliens. Although the guards draw their guns, they are easily overtaken by the soldiers.

A Confederate major steps forward and approaches the Detention Center's administrator, "This facility is now under the control of the Confederate Army. Effective immediately, you are all prisoners. This building is completely surrounded. If you surrender, your men's lives will be saved."

The administrator responds, "We don't work for the military, and you are not part of the American army. You are rebels and you are all under arrest."

"I think not." The Major pulls out his pistol and shoots the administrator in the head. All of the Major's men draw their guns. "Anybody else?" threatens the Major.

The detention guards drop their guns.

The Major, "All right men gather the illegals. They're all going back to Mexico."

At the White House in the Oval Office, President Wilson admits to Hunter, "I never thought it would come to this."

Hunter responds, "Sir, we should consider that we could face an attack on the east coast within a few days."

"What makes you say that?"

"Because that's what I would do. We need to prepare a defense of D.C. and the White House. If they capture this building it's a great victory for them, even if you're able to escape. Susan Crane will deliver a victory speech from the East Room, announcing to the world that you are no longer the President"

"What about our nuclear weapons?"

Hunter assures him, "Everything has been secured."

"And the investigation, do we have any leads?"

Hunter responds, "I'm meeting with Beeks and Collins later today."

The President tells Hunter, "Just keep me informed."

A CNN broadcast shows Confederate soldiers escorting Mexican Americans across the border back into Mexico. Stanley continues, "As this struggle moves into its second week, it appears that Confederate soldiers have taken control of all major cities in the southwest with the exception of Los Angeles. We have learned that Los Angeles is being protected by the California National Guard and two armored Marine divisions."

"With their military success, the Confederate government has enacted a series of laws imposing social changes in keeping with their political views." On the screen, Planned Parenthood facilities are shown surrounded by Confederate soldiers and being closed. "In a statement issued by Governor Crane's office earlier today, the Confederacy has placed a ban on abortion, repealed federal taxes for anyone making over one million dollars a year, and issued an

Executive Order giving illegal aliens two weeks to leave the U.S. or face 'aggressive state action' -- whatever that means. Also, all US attorneys in states under confederated control have been replaced by Governor Crane's appointees."

Watching TV in the Crane living room report their success, Calvin Crane, Andrew Mellon, and Skip Garrison are celebrating with drinks. Susan walks in, "What's up gentlemen?"

Her husband responds, "General Baxter informed us that we are ready to begin the advance on Washington tomorrow."

She suggests, "I think we should wait. They're weak. We can probably negotiate a good deal and get what we want."

Mellon doesn't want to hear any of this, "I, and before me my father, have been running the Republican Party for more than a century. We built this country, financed two world wars and defeated the Soviets. We've eliminated and impeached presidents, framed senators and removed judges, and we only got caught once thanks to Nixon. If I say we go tomorrow, we go tomorrow. There's nothing to negotiate. When we're in the White House, they'll negotiate with us."

Calvin looks at Susan for her reaction as she replies, "I don't really know what you're talking about but I'll go along...for now."

Mellon instructs Susan, "If you want to meet with Wilson then do it, but use our leverage. He either makes you number two or he resigns. I really don't care which. He won't run again anyway, so if he wants to be President for a couple years, fine, as long as he knows we call the shots."

In Collins' office at FBI Headquarters, Hunter, Collins, and Beeks discuss the investigation. Collins offers, "We're pretty sure this was not Islamic terrorists."

Hunter asks, "What leads you to believe that?"

Collins answers, "Well sir, we have the truck driver who delivered the bomb to the Capitol in custody, and the information he provided eventually led us to a DC lawyer named Garrison, Skip Garrison."

Hunter, "I know him. He's with Ropes and something. Walsh or Welsh."

She clarifies, "Welsh, sir."

Beeks says, "Jimmy, the bottom line is that while the explosive devices probably came from overseas, the conspiracy was domestic."

Collins continues, "Sir, I was in the Persian Gulf and I saw the bomb materials there. Those specific parts are all needed to cause such extensive damage using the type of explosives FBI forensics say were detonated at the Capital. The only problem is that while the bomb components could easily get through customs, how the hell did it get through security at the Capital?"

Hunter, "Who are your suspects?"

Beeks answers, "Well, Garrison and the President are old friends from their college days."

"What are you suggesting?"

Collins, "He's not the only one who is connected to Garrison. Calvin Crane also knew him well."

Hunter asks, "So now what?

Collins responds nodding to Beeks, "We will continue investigating."

As he leaves Collins' office Hunter advises, "Make it quick because the country is on the brink of war."

Collins and Beeks are left alone in the office.

Collins, "Hunter's right you know."

"About what?"

"About everything," she explains. "I mean either President Wilson was behind it, or he knew about it, or those responsible made sure that Wilson wasn't going to be at the State of the Union speech." Pondering, "Or maybe he's being framed – but by who, and for what reason?"

"If he wasn't a part of the conspiracy then why did they select him?"

She suggests, "Because they felt they could influence him because he's a Republican, or they already controlled him. For all we know, they have some pictures of him with a teenage girl or even juicier, maybe he 'trumped' several of them at once."

"And in this grand conspiracy of yours who is 'they'?"

The next day on the radio, "Good morning New York. It's 6am and time for your world headlines. The stock market has stabilized. Yesterday the DOW closed down only two percent, the smallest decline since the State of the Union tragedy."

In Washington DC it is also a beautiful morning. Grounds crews are working at the White House as construction workers are clearing out debris from the Capitol. In the distance across the Potomac River, a plane lands at Reagan Airport. It pulls into a hanger. Susan Crane and Skip Garrison exit the plane surrounded by body guards and aides. The two enter a limo and the motorcade leaves.

The radio report continues, "The White House has announced that a meeting between President Wilson and Governor Crane will take place this morning to consider how best to resolve this national tragedy."

At a coffee shop in Washington DC, Beeks and Collins enjoy a morning cup of java. Collins' phone rings, "Hello. Really? All right, secure him there." She asks Beeks, "Guess who just showed up at his Office?

"Who?"

"Garrison. They've placed him under guard and await further instructions."

At the White House, Susan Crane enters the Oval Office and shakes President Wilson's hand. "Good morning John. Good of you to see me on such short notice."

"Hello Susan. Thanks for coming. We've certainly gotten ourselves into one big mess."

They both sit down. Crane bodyguard and two Secret Service agents are the only other people in the room.

The President continues, "I'll get right to the point. The Federal government will grant your rebels immunity so long as your army ceases all military actions. For the sake of the country and the world, this conflict needs to end now."

"Appoint me Vice President, maintain the Executive Orders we've introduced, and you have a deal."

The President is about to say something, but he thinks for a moment. He then nods his head in the affirmative. Susan interjects, "You also must agree not to run in four years."

He asks, "Do I have a choice?"

She responds, "Even if you run and win, you will never serve a second term, and you know it. You didn't play ball when you should have. It's out of my hands now and you know whose hands it's in."

At his law firm, Skip Garrison is sitting on the couch in his office with a guard stationed outside his door. Collins knocks. As Beeks and Collins enter, she asks, "Do you want to take the lead here or do you want me to handle this?"

Beeks responds, "I've got it." Collins smiles as he begins, "Mr. Garrison, we've been dying to talk to you."

Skip asks, "Who are you? What can I do for you?"

"This is Natalie Collins with the FBI and I'm..."

Collins interrupts him, "We're investigating the Capitol bombing and your name keeps coming up."

"I don't know how. I wasn't even in Washington..."

Beeks points at him, "You were the middle man between Calvin Crane and the people responsible for the bombing of the Capitol and killing and maiming hundreds of people. Not to mention that it was you who got that SUV into the Capitol complex."

Garrison replies, "I don't know what you're talking about."

Collins stops him, "Mr. Garrison, don't bullshit us. We know what you did, we can prove it, and unless you start cooperating, you'll get the needle."

Beeks, "I have to say that even if you do cooperate, you could get the needle. Mass murder is serious business."

Collins, "My partner here is concerned about where the bomb came from, but I care more about who paid you and convinced you to do it. If Calvin Crane isn't behind this, who is?" She pauses and gives him a 'you're caught' look. "Try to imagine a needle in your arm."

He collapses and admits, "It was John Wilson."

FBI agents escort Garrison in handcuffs out to the street, through a crowd of protestors and reporters, to a waiting SUV. Beeks is stunned by the development that the attack was perpetrated by President Wilson, "Well, we're certainly in over our heads now."

Collins looks at him like he's a rookie, "You know he's lying. Wilson never planned this."

Beeks tells her, "We still need to interview the President, and right now. This story is going to break big."

Collins, "Well Garrison sure didn't deny Calvin Crane's involvement. But if it wasn't President Wilson, who the hell is he protecting?"

In the Oval Office, the President and Governor Crane are still negotiating, "the bottom line, Susan, is that I can't do it. The American Presidency is far too important to be bargained nor negotiated. It is not a pawn, and neither am I. I don't know how or why this all began, but we will get to the bottom of it, I promise you."

She is ruthless, "Well, according to our investigative services, it seems clear that you hired Skip Garrison to arrange for the bombing of the Capitol. Once everyone learns that, they will side with me."

"That is a lie and the press would never believe it."

Susan stands up and walks out of the Oval Office, "Too late Mr. Former President."

She passes an aide who walks in and whispers something to the President. The President tells the aide, "Turn it on." The Aide turns on the TV.

Stanley Ropert is reporting the breaking news. 'America: The Civil War' appears on the bottom of the screen, "As we continue our live continuous coverage of "America: The Civil War", we bring you these live shots of noted Washington DC attorney Skip Garrison being arrested at his downtown office."

The President tells his aide, "Get Hunter on the phone."

"Yes sir, Mr. President. FBI agent Collins and NSA agent Beeks are here to see you."

"Show them in."

In a Las Vegas hotel suite that is set up like a military command center, General Baxter is on the phone, "Calvin, what did your wife say."

"She met with Wilson and he said no. Prepare to launch against the east coast immediately."

Beeks and Collins enter the Oval Office. The President stands with his back to them staring out the window at the Rose Garden.

He tells them, "Come in. Andrew I thought you were with the CIA?"

"Good morning Sir. I've been officially transferred to the NSA due to this domestic issue. I legally can't work this investigation while at the CIA."

The President, "I hope you're not torturing anybody."

Beeks doesn't say a word.

The President asks, "How we doing? What's the status of the investigation?"

Collins, "We assume you heard about Skip Garrison's arrest."

Beeks, "That was us, Sir."

Collins gives Beeks a 'shut up' look.

The President offers, "You know he was my classmate at Yale."

Beeks, "We know, Sir."

Collins, "That's what we want to speak to you about."

"Sure. Sit down." They do. The President continues, "We went to Yale together, Law school, fraternity, the whole thing."

Collins inquires, "What about Calvin Crane, did you know him at Yale?"

"Yeah, we were all in law school together. Do you think he's involved?

Beeks, "We can't say for certain, but it's possible."

The President, "Well let's not ignore the elephant in the middle of the Oval Office. Do you suspect me?

Beeks, "Garrison fingered you."

"What? Why would he do that?"

Collins offers an explanation, "We don't know yet, but we think he's full of crap. We think he's protecting someone in addition to Calvin Crane. They apparently think framing you strengthens their cause."

Howard Mellon's mansion is enormous – it is like combining the Titanic and the White House. Guests arrive as bodyguards with machine guns stand spread throughout the grounds. The driveway is over a mile long and there are several helicopters on the front lawn from which men in beautiful traditional white Arab attire exit. They are surrounded by their own bodyguards.

In a sitting room, Susan, Calvin, and Howard Mellon sit quietly while Calvin is on the phone, "Very good General Baxter." As he hangs up the phone, "Baxter will attack Washington tomorrow."

Mellon turns to Susan, "Well then it's time to make good on your threat Susan"

She suggests, "Maybe I should call Wilson again."

She picks up the phone, but Mellon demands, "Put the phone down. Nobody is calling anyone."

Susan explains, "I didn't think it was a 'take it or leave it' offer. I thought we were negotiating."

Mellon tells Calvin, "Can't you control your wife?"

"I don't need controlling."

Calvin, "Honey, you need to understand."

Susan interrupts him, "Shut up Calvin."

Mellon reflects, "She doesn't know, does she? You never told her."

"Told me what?"

Mellon reveals the truth, "Skip Garrison wasn't hired by Wilson. Your husband hired him."

"What?"

"Tell her Calvin."

Susan yells, "What did you do?"

Mellon, "Tell her. She already knows or she should if she's smart. The real question is, does the President know that she knows?"

Susan is visually upset, and says to her husband in a stricken voice, "Some of our closest friends were in that building."

Mellon interrupts, "They were casualties of war."

Calvin stands up and pours himself a scotch as Susan raises her voice, "Calvin, you better say something, god-dammit. We're all going to jail for murder."

Calvin ignores her as Mellon explains, "Nobody is going to jail. This has nothing to do with crime. It has to do with politics and patriotism. We are putting America first. The United States killed hundreds of thousands, maybe even millions, in Iraq and the Middle East and do you think any American will ever be charged with war crimes? In the meantime, we killed that son of a bitch Saddam Hussein and convinced world leaders that he had committed war crimes –

and at the same time, convinced most Americans that he was the one who attacked us on 9/11."

Several Mellon bodyguards knock and enter the room and stand in front of the only door, blocking it. Mellon continues, "You see my dear, whoever controls the media, the propaganda machine, as it's sometimes negatively called, controls the world."

One of Mellon's men says, "Mr. Mellon, Prince Ali has arrived."

He concludes, "This is not the first time we've had to take drastic measures to maintain our freedom and the American way of life."

Susan asks, "And what way is that Howard?"

"It's my way." Mellon stands up and walks towards the door where his men are standing post. More bodyguards walk in.

Calvin tells Susan, "Sweetie, I was gonna tell you."

Mellon, "You are a part of history, both of you. That's because I create history. But don't forget that I can also re-write it. Susan, if you don't screw this up, you may just become the first woman President of the United States. Think of it, it's hard to believe that the first female vice president will not be a Democrat. Like I said, I create history."

Another bodyguard enters and says, "Mr. Mellon, General Baxter is on the phone for you."

Mellon instructs his men, "Our guests will be staying here with us for a little while. Please make sure they are safe and not disturbed by anyone. They need some time to think and to grow up."

"Yes sir," his men reply, and address Susan and Calvin, "We're going to need your cell phones."

As Mellon leaves the room, "The two of you, get your shit together." His men close the door and walk toward Susan and Calvin, who meekly hand over their cell phones.

"Governor Crane, please stand-up so we can search you."

Humiliated, she does.

At the White House, Secret Service agents, police officers, and soldiers are standing post. Many have machine guns drawn. German shepherds are barking. Tanks and armored vehicles are stationed in front of the gates. American soldiers continue to arrive by the truck-load.

In the Oval Office, Beeks asks the President, "What about the other guys you went to school with?"

Collins adds, "Besides you, who else was close with both Garrison and Calvin Crane?"

The President, "Nobody."

Beeks, "Come on, don't bullshit us. We know someone else has to be involved pulling the strings."

Surprised by his language, the President gives him a look of shock - so does Collins.

"Andrew Mellon," says the President.

Beeks asks, "Who is he?"

"He's the heir to the Mellon fortune," Collins responds. "Oil, gas, steel, shipping."

Beeks, "Why would he be involved?"

Collins nods her head in the affirmative, "Because..."

"Because his family, along with another hundred or so industrialists and financiers, control the Republican Party," interrupts the President. "They call themselves conservatives, though they're really not. They don't give a damn about illegal immigration, gun control, or gay marriage. They take those positions to appeal to voters. At the end of the day, they want lower taxes for their friends, less government oversight over their businesses, and control of the world economy."

Collins, "Well I wouldn't have put it like that."

"Mellon is very dangerous," the President adds, "and if he is behind this, and he knows you can prove it, you'll never find him and your lives are in grave danger."

Beeks, "We probably can prove it, given enough time."

Wilson expresses great frustration, "We've run out of time. I'm about to be framed by Susan Crane for blowing up the Capitol – and the press is playing right into their hands."

THE WHITE HOUSE

The world looks on anxiously as the siege on Washington DC is imminent. Worldwide, stock markets are in shambles. For the first time since the tragedy at the Capitol, the sun can't be seen this morning. The clouds gather as Confederate soldiers armed with tanks and Humvees race toward the Potomac. General Baxter stands on the street next to his jeep looking like General George Patton, cheering on his troops as they march by.

The radio reports, "At dawn in Washington DC, our lead story is that talks between Governor Crane and President Wilson have reportedly broken down, and that Confederate forces are less than ten miles from the Potomac River, ready to cross into Washington DC."

In the sky Confederate F-15s fly toward Washington preparing to attack. At the same time, inside the Operations Center at the NMCC, Major O'Connor hangs up the phone and reports to Fitzgerald and Hunter, "The Pentagon is secure. We have several thousand troops in the city with two divisions coming in tonight from North Carolina. They will be able to counter attack in the morning if we lose the city. We will engage the F-15s in thirty seconds."

In the airspace above Washington D.C. Super Hornets under Hunter's command are flying over the Potomac preparing to engage Confederate F-15s.

"Sir, do we have permission to engage?" the Hornet Commander asks NMCC.

"That's affirmative, Commander."

Hornet Commander, "F-15 Eagle commander, this is the US Air Force, please identify yourself. You have entered secured air space. Divert now."

No response.

"Please identify yourself or we will engage. Again, divert now."

No response.

Hornet Commander, "OK gentlemen. Prepare to engage. Lock on targets - fire."

The Hornets fire. The missiles move toward the F-15s. Several are hit. The F-15s fire back. The Hornets greatly outnumber the F-15s. One F-15 gets through and is heading toward the White House.

NMCC on the radio, "One got through. One got through Commander."

"I see him. I got tone. Fire three."

The Commander's Hornet fires and hits the F-15. It crashes on the Washington Mall as the Hornet flies over the Washington Monument.

Everyone cheers at NMCC as Major O'Connor, Hunter, and Fitzgerald watch the camera view of the Hornet as it flies over the Mall. But then an alarm sounds. "What's that?" asks O'Connor.

A Sergeant responds, "Enemy F-15s forty miles outside of mid-town Manhattan."

Fitzgerald asks, "How many?"

Sergeant, "Over twenty-five."

Hunter screams, "Scramble two more squadrons of Hornets from Teterboro now!"

In the New York City airspace, Confederate F-15s are flying toward Manhattan as Hunter's Hornets take off.

A Lieutenant in the cockpit of the lead Hornet hears his instructions over the radio, "This is NMCC, you have about twenty-five F-15s twenty miles south of the city - permission to engage."

The Hornet Lieutenant, "That's affirmative."

The Hornets and the F-15s are flying right toward one another.

F-15 Commander, "Red team lock on targets and prepare to fire." His weapons systems screen shows the Empire State building as the target, "Fire."

The F-15s fire their missiles. The missiles hit their targets in lower Manhattan -- one missile hits the Empire State Building.

At NMCC, Major O'Connor informs Hunter, "The Empire State Building was just hit."

Hornet Lieutenant, "Fire." The Hornets fire and most of the F-15s are hit. The remaining F-15s fly away.

At the Potomac River, the only bridge still standing is the Arlington Memorial Bridge. General Baxter is on the Virginia side in between the river and Arlington National Cemetery while the American soldiers are on the other at the western tip of the Washington Mall surrounding the Lincoln Memorial. An aide approaches Baxter who stands right outside his Humvee, "Our F-15s in New York are retreating south."

Baxter asks, "What did they hit?"

His aide, "Lower Manhattan is on fire and we hit the Empire State building."

In Manhattan, people are running through the streets just like on 9/11. On CNN Stanley Ropert sits in the anchor chair, "You are looking at live shots from lower Manhattan. As you can see, there is wide-spread destruction"

At The White House, Secret Service agents rush past the President's secretary and into the Oval Office. Hunter's top SEAL commander, Colonel Tanner, enters the room as the agents surround the President. Everyone watches CNN, replaying over and over again, people running for their lives on the streets of New York and the Empire State Building on fire.

Colonel Tanner, "Mr. President, Chairman Hunter has ordered your immediate evacuation. Please come with us."

"I'm not leaving."

"Sir, General Baxter is only miles away." Tanner insists, "We have no more time."

"If I leave, the next picture will be Susan Crane sitting in this chair on TV establishing presidential policy. I'm staying."

Tanner speaks into his radio, "NMCC command, this is Colonel Tanner with the President. He is a no go. Repeat he is a no go. Please advise."

At NMCC Hunter asks, "What did he say?"

Standing next to him, Major O'Connor repeats, "He says President Wilson is staying."

"All right," Hunter responds. "Move the 53rd Rangers from the Capitol to sixteen hundred. Get the chopper ready and tell The President that I'll be there in five minutes."

As Hunter begins running out, Beeks shouts, "Wait!" Hunter stops. "I'm coming too."

"So am I," adds Collins as they all run out toward the waiting chopper.

Lower Manhattan is on fire. In midtown, people race out of the Empire State Building as Stanley Ropert continues to report on the attack. "As we watch these incredible images from Manhattan, we have received an unconfirmed report that President Wilson is being investigated by the FBI for the bombing of the Capitol. Sources at the conservative American Values Council have issued a statement substantiating these findings."

At the Potomac River, Baxter's Confederate troops are being engaged by American soldiers. The Americans are overwhelmed by Baxter's tanks. The Confederates cross the river, securing the other side passing several destroyed tanks and dead American soldiers.

As Hunter's chopper lands on the White House grounds, Secret Service agents guard every door to the White House. American soldiers and tanks have surrounded the White House with guns pointed toward the Potomac. One mile from the White House, Confederate troops are only a few blocks away from the Washington Monument.

Hunter, Beeks and Collins head to the Oval Office to brief the President. As they speak among themselves Collins, "We're convinced it was Skip Garrison and Calvin Crane, probably backed by Andrew Mellon."

"Andrew Mellon is one of the richest men in America," says the President, "Why would he be involved?"

"Greed, narcissism, power – what's the difference?" replies Beeks.

Collins asks, "The question is how involved was Governor Crane?"

"What do you think?" Hunter counters.

"From a legal point of view we don't need to flip Crane to make our case. From a non-legal point of view, it's not my place to provide political advice."

Hunter, "Beeks, I know, you can't hold your opinion back."

"She probably knew after the fact," he answers. "My sense is that her husband and his old pal Mellon were manipulating her. Garrison was just the operative to procure the bomb and get it into the Capitol where it could do the most damage."

Collins adds, "The bottom line is motive, and these guys and their parents and grandparents before them have been manipulating politics and the US government since World War II; Cuba, Kennedy in Dallas, Nixon and the break-in, Iran Contra, Monica Lewinsky and Ken Starr, the Iraq War, Trump and Russia. The only difference is that this time they got caught. Or we will catch them soon enough."

As they reach the door to the Oval Office, Hunter concludes, "Here and now, we have a civil war threatening our nation's future, and here and now, we need to stop it. Then we'll get Calvin, Mellon and everyone else who played a role in this disaster."

Hunter, Beeks and Collins enter. The President is sitting at his desk surrounded by Secret Service agents with additional agents covering the exits. Hunter instructs Beeks and Collins, "Just get the correct story out there in the media as quickly as possible. If they blame the President and it sticks, we're all finished."

The President overhears what Hunter is saying, "What about the media?"

He responds, "We've definitely proven that two of your fellow Yalies are behind this and are also responsible for the bombing of the Capitol. Beeks and Collins can prove it. But if the wrong story gets out there, you're done."

"How can you be sure?"

"Look who's behind the blackmail," Hunter suggests.

Collins ads, "Only the blackmailer could really know what and how it happened."

The President is shocked, "Governor Susan Crane?

Hunter, "She's the only one who is blackmailing you to accept her conditions."

The President asks, "But why?"

Just then a massive explosion over the parks and gardens somewhere near the Washington Monument can be seen through the windows. Secret Service agents shield the President. Just outside the Oval Office, soldiers, police officers and Secret Service agents run south toward the southern gates, the Ellipse, and the Washington Monument.

On CNN, Stanley Ropert is in the anchor chair, "This just in - Governor Crane's Confederate troops are now only a mile from the White House."

In the CNN control room, producer Kelly is on the phone, "All right Rob, let's go live. Interrupt Stanley. Just start – speak!"

Rob Black, "I'm moving through the White House, and can see that Confederate forces led by General Baxter have reached the Washington Mall." Explosions echo throughout the city as he continues, "The President is still inside the Oval Office protected by Secret Service agents."

In the Oval Office an agent says, "Sir, we have to move now!"

Hunter adds, "Mr. President, we need to move you to a secure location immediately. We can evacuate you now. Sir, we need to maintain a working government."

Beeks adds, "Sir, Collins is on the phone with the networks right now. Her proof will break the case wide open, but we need you to still be alive or their coup d'etat will succeed."

Collins on the phone, "Yes, Kelly. That's right. He was framed. I'm texting you the proof right now."

Kelly asks Collins, "Is Governor Crane a suspect?"

Collins responds, "She is more than a suspect. She will be arrested for conspiracy and we are also issuing arrest warrants for her husband and for Howard Mellon. We believe Mellon bank-rolled the whole thing, or at least that's where the evidence points."

For the next two hours, Rob Black at the White House, and Stanley Ropert at CNN headquarters, in Atlanta broadcasted the only live coverage of the attack on the White House. It was like 1991, all over again when Bernard Shaw, Peter Arnett, and John Holliman were the only journalists reporting live from Baghdad at the beginning of the first Gulf War. The other networks had either been cut off or were reporting that the Confederated States could prove to the world that President Wilson was guilty. A civil war had begun and they were reporting that if the President were to step down, the country could unite. Some reports suggested that the President had been captured and that clemency had been offered in exchange for resigning. However, one person was standing all alone on the Truman Balcony of the White House overlooking the South Lawn – Rob Black.

At CNN, Kelly's team gets her attention when it is quite clear that all the channels are carrying the CNN feed. The monitors broadcasting live pictures from within the White House are all from Rob's cell phone.

"I can see him now in the distance -- General Baxter is standing in front of his mechanized units. I can even see some tanks. The American soldiers seem to be withdrawing behind the White House itself. Wow, did you just see that? It was like a giant flashbang. We are lit up by flood lights. I think they're coming."

He continues, "Can you hear that gunfire? Now we're hearing a lot of gunfire. Small arms fire, but a lot. Alright, they are moving. General Baxter is leading his troops toward the White House. Those were definitely explosions on the South Lawn. Oh my God, that explosion must have killed 30 secret service agents. Baxter's tanks have just blown through the outer perimeter and it looks like the soldiers are entering the White House grounds. The agents are withdrawing back to the West Wing. They are completely overpowered. There seems to be a pause now in the gunfire. I've gotta move."

Stanley, "Be careful there Rob. Get someplace safe. I will just recap that this is live video of a Confederate battalion of mechanized and armored units. In some of this video it looks like the battalion has split in two -- half flanking left and the other to the right. Most importantly, according to our sources, and contradictory to what most other news outlets are saying, we can confirm that the President has not been captured"

"I'm back Stanley. Can you hear me?"

"Yes, go ahead Rob. What do you see?"

"I had to move away from the railing but I'm still outside. The entire second floor here seems to be empty. But I still see agents all around. I can see the Oval Office. I have to move closer. Can you see this? I can look through the glass and see – I'll show you. There are many agents and marine guards surrounding the West Wing. There are also many agents outside the Oval Office. Their guns are all out. It looks like they are taking up defensive positions."

In the Oval Office, everyone has their guns drawn. Senior military officers enter the room with brief cases, including the "football" with the nuclear codes.

Collins hangs up the phone and nods to Hunter who says, "Mr. President, it's time."

As the President rises from his chair and moves toward the doors, a missile hits the Oval Office. It explodes but the bullet-proof glass does not shatter. The Secret Service agents jump on the President to protect him. Collins draws her gun. So does Hunter. The agents move the President out of the Oval Office as Colonel Tanner leads the way into the adjacent reception area.

On the South Lawn outside the West Wing, Secret Service agents have their machine guns drawn. As Baxter's Confederate troops approach them, they are quickly overpowered.

Rob continues reporting from the Truman Balcony, "I can see the remaining agents running for cover back into the West Wing. There are some on the roof of the West Wing. Confederate troops are heading toward me now, still firing on the agents. The President appears to be trapped between the Oval Office and the Cabinet Room. I can see flashes from the Cabinet Room."

Stanley, "Are Confederate troops in the West Wing? Rob, are you still there?"

Rob, "I can't move and I must stay quiet. The troops have entered the White House and are outside on the West Colonnade and in the Briefing Room firing on those last agents protecting the President. It cannot be long now as Confederate soldiers are converging from three sides – from the South Lawn, from across the Rose Garden and now from the north where the press offices are. Something is happening now. I can see the President through the windows. Can you see that? This may be it. The President may be forced to surrender at any moment."

Just then a fresh team of Secret Service agents exit from the Oval Office and begin firing on the Confederate forces. Unfortunately they too are outnumbered. Hunter sees this and bursts out of one of the glass doors shooting at Baxter's men and shouting to the few remaining agents, "Get the President out of here right now."

The agents, headed by Colonel Tanner and Collins, move the President from the secretary's office into the hallway. They are quickly met by Baxter and his Confederate troops who fire on them from the other end of the hall. A shot is fired. Tanner is down. The Secret Service agents grab the President and push him back into the secretary's office. Collins gets off several shots before grabbing Tanner and taking cover behind the door.

Hunter, "What happening?"

"Four men at the end of the corridor," Collins responds. "I think one of them is Baxter."

While still firing through the open door at Confederate troops in the Rose Garden, Hunter looks down at Tanner, "Is he okay?"

"He will be," responds one of the agents.

Hunter, "You need to get out of here now. I can't hold these guys off forever."

Beeks draws his gun and joins Hunter at the door. Collins tells the agents, "All right you are with me. We'll clear the hall. If we don't get the President through that hall and out of the lobby quickly, we're all dead." The agents and Collins enter the hallway shooting at Baxter and his men. With adrenaline pumping, they enter the hallway killing the Confederate soldiers at the other end. "Hunter, we're clear let's go."

Collins and the agents run down the hallway but within a few steps, they are again under Confederate fire. The agents take cover back in the secretary's office to protect the President.

On CNN Stanley Ropert is reporting. "Rob, I don't know if you can hear me? Can you hear me, Rob? Okay we seem to have lost him so I will recap. What we know now is that the White House is under attack by Confederate soldiers and that Secret Service agents are trying to evacuate the President. We have been able to see and hear the incredible explosions coming from the West Wing. We understand that the President wanted to stay at the White House against the advice of the military and Secret Service, and that it may too late for an evacuation. Confederate troops outnumber the

Secret Service agents, and we believe that the President may be trapped in the halls of the White House."

In the hall just outside the Cabinet Room, Secret Service agents are shooting at the Confederate soldiers. Collins and Beeks also fire in a barrage but the soldiers return fire, hitting some agents. From the secretary's office, one of the Secret Service agents hands Hunter a Rocket Propelled Grenade. Hunter quickly jumps in front of the cross fire and fires it. A large explosion kills all the Confederate soldiers in the hallway, including Baxter, and in the process, takes out the wall behind them. Before the smoke even begins to clear, Hunter orders, "Move the President out to the car."

"Evac everyone now," Beeks shouts. The agents run out through the hole in the wall surrounding the President who moves with them.

In the CNN control room, producer Kelly is typing on her computer while on the phone and tells her team, "All right, we're going with this breaking news." Pointing to her computer, she tells the Assistant Director, "Tell Stanley to read this - now."

Secret Service agents and American soldiers are protecting the north-western driveway. The President exits the West Wing surrounded by agents led by Collins, "Let's go, let's go. Get him in!" Once the President is rushed into a black SUV it speeds off with other Secret Service SUVs and police cars exiting the grounds, still taking fire from the remaining Confederate soldiers.

In the newsroom, Kelly is drinking coffee pacing back and forth in front of her monitor. Her Assistant Director is becoming more and more nervous as Kelly asks, "Are we going to get this to Stanley or should I..."

"Three seconds. OK. Go."

Kelly, "Stanley, go - read it,"

On worldwide live TV, he unprofessionally asks Kelly, "Are you sure?"

"Yes God dammit. Read it now!"

He begins, "CNN has confirmed that the report issued by the American Family Council an hour ago and broadcast on all major conservative news outlets, is false. We understand that the Director of the FBI and their key investigative team will hold a press conference outlining their evidence and we will join them live in about fifteen minutes. In the meantime, we have received confirmation from several federal officials that there is strong evidence that previous reports that the bombing at the Capital was orchestrated by President Wilson are false. I repeat, those reports appear to be false. In fact, we expect the announcement by the FBI to confirm that the bombing of the Capitol was the first stage of a coup d'état planned by one of the wealthiest men in the world, Pittsburgh steel tycoon Howard Mellon."

Within the hour, FBI agents, SWAT teams, and police officers approach the Mellon Mansion. Armored vehicles move toward the house. Several armed henchmen loyal to

Mellon are protecting the front door. Using silencers, the agents and SWAT team fire at Mellon's men and kill them.

The images on CNN show Mellon and several aides being escorted out of the house by FBI agents. Stanley reports, "A federal arrest warrant has been issued for Howard Mellon. Arrest warrants have also been issued for Governor Susan Crane and her husband Calvin Crane."

One Month Later

President Wilson is at his desk when Hunter enters the room and stands in front of him.

"Good morning, Jimmy."

"Good morning Mr. President."

"Good to see you again and well. So where are we?"

"We rounded them all up: Calvin Crane, Howard Mellon, even General Baxter may pull through. The Attorney General told me that grand jury indictments will be handed down before the end of the day -- for murder, treason and espionage – the works."

"And what of the others?"

"Who would that be?" asks Hunter.

"The millions who went along with them, who wanted to divide the Union."

"For what? What was their crime?" Hunter thinks for a moment and then adds, "What did Lincoln do one-hundred and fifty years ago? Didn't he allow all of them, Union and Confederate alike, to go back to their families?"

"What happened to Robert E. Lee, although only a general, and The Confederate President then were radically different"

Hunter, "Almost no one even knows the name Jefferson Davis."

"Ironic, isn't it? History teaches us that Lee had not only accepted the loss in the South, but did more to encourage southerners to move on than Lincoln could have ever done."

"Meanwhile, Davis lived in denial after prison and ultimately died a lonely man."

The President, "I spoke with the new Speaker of the House this morning. The House and the Senate are committed to reuniting the country. The American people need healing and so I spoke with him about the VP post."

Hunter asks, "Was he interested?"

"I didn't ask him. I told him that I would be picking a leader and not a politician." The President rises from his chair and walks around his desk to Hunter. He reaches out his hand. "You interested?"

"I serve at your pleasure, Mr. President," as they shake hands.

One Year Later

At FBI Headquarters Collins is on the phone when Beeks walks in. "Yes sir, I'll tell him. He just walked in. Thank you, sir. Good night." She hangs up the phone.

"Who was that?"

"The President."

Beeks looks surprised, "So you speak to him directly now."

"It's unbelievable."

"What?"

"How jealous you are."

"I'm not jealous."

"First you definitely are jealous. Second, you were thinking that you were going to spend the night with me."

"What? Who? Me?"

"Yeah, I know how you think – and you're right. You are going to spend the night."

"Really?"

"We're going to the State of the Union. Then the President wants us on a plane to the Middle East tomorrow morning to track more missing nuclear materials. The satellite got a fix on two possible locations in the Persian Gulf. The SEAL team will meet us at Andrews tomorrow morning."

She puts on her coat, "Flights at Oh-four-hundred. Try not to be late."

"I'm not getting up that early."

"You're not getting up at all. We're working all night. You can sleep on the plane."

He's standing at the door. It's open. She walks toward him and says "By the way, what did Hunter say about me?"

"He said beware – she's smarter than you."

"What a nice compliment. Let's pick up dinner on the way. What do you want, McDonalds or Burger King."

He looks at her like she's crazy, "You're kidding right?"

"Don't worry. I'll get burgers from Burger King and fries from McDonalds."

At the White House, the door to the Oval Office opens and in walks Henry Johnson, the Secretary of Education. President Wilson is sitting at his desk, looking relaxed and relieved that the crisis of the Civil War has been averted, and the nation is again united. He is enjoying a fine cigar, "Hank, come in." He rises and walks over to Johnson and shakes his hand.

"Good evening, Mr. President."

"As you know, a cabinet member is normally asked to remain in the Oval Office during the speech, but since we're doing the State of the Union from the White House tonight, I think it would be best if you were at the Pentagon."

Johnson looks nervous, "That sounds fine to me, sir."

"Don't worry - everything is going to be fine."

Covering the event on CNN from his anchor chair is Stanley Ropert. "We have been informed by the White House that security has been especially tight for the past three days in preparation for the President's State of the Union Address. And of course, given the events of one year ago, no one is surprised. We now go to White House correspondent Rob Black who is there."

Rob, "Here at 1600 Pennsylvania Avenue, several tents have been erected creating one large tent on the South Lawn. It is large enough to hold one thousand people. Security is obviously very tight, with everyone walking through metal detectors and there are Secret Service agents everywhere, along with more members of the media than I ever remember being assembled here at the White House"

Stanley, "The President is only seconds away and the crowd has become quiet -- here he comes."

The doors to the White House are closed, and Secret Service agents stand post on either side. The doors open and several more agents exit the White House followed by the President. They enter the tent following the Crier, "Here ye, here ye. Mr. Speaker, the President of the United States."

The President enters. Everyone rises and applauds. He begins...

EPILOGUE

Almost everywhere we look, the story is the same. In Latin America, in Africa, in Asia, in the councils of the world and in the jungles of far-off nations, there is now renewed confidence in our country and our convictions.

For this country is moving and it must not stop. It cannot stop. For this is a time for courage and a time for challenge. Neither conformity nor complacency will do. Neither the fanatics nor the faint-hearted are needed. And our duty as a party is not to our party alone, but to the Nation, and, indeed, to all mankind. Our duty is not merely the preservation of political power but the preservation of peace and freedom.

So let us not be petty when our cause is so great. Let us not quarrel amongst ourselves when our Nation's future is at stake. Let us stand together with renewed confidence in our cause − united in our heritage of the past and our Hopes for the future − and determine that this land we love shall lead all mankind into new frontiers of peace and abundance.

(Remarks intended for delivery to the Texas Democratic State Committee in the Municipal Auditorium in Austin, Texas by President John F. Kennedy. November 22, 1963.)

Added in the Special Impeachment Edition originally the Epilogue from The Mueller Report Uncertainty – A Treatise on the Victims of Narcissism.

I learned long ago that when there are no words, find someone else's. This is read by Rabbi Paul Shrell-Fox before Yizkor (Memorial Service) at my synagogue on Yom Kippur. (writer/original source unknown)

THE PARADOX OF OUR TIME in history is that we have taller buildings but shorter tempers, wider freeways, but narrower viewpoints. We spend more, but have less, we buy more, but enjoy less. We have bigger houses and smaller families, more conveniences, but less time. We have more degrees but less sense, more knowledge, but less judgment, more experts, yet more problems, more medicine, but less wellness. We drink too much, smoke too much, spend too recklessly, laugh too little, drive too fast, get too angry, stay up too late, get up too tired, read too little, watch TV too much, and pray too seldom. We have multiplied our possessions, but reduced our values. We talk too much, love too seldom, and hate too often. We've learned how to make a living, but not a life. We've added years to life not life to years. We've been all the way to the moon and back, but have trouble crossing the street to meet a new neighbor. We conquered outer space but not inner space. We've done larger things, but not better things. We've cleaned up the air, but polluted the soul. We've conquered the atom, but not our prejudice. We write more, but learn less. We plan more, but accomplish less. We've learned to rush, but not to wait. We build more computers to hold more information, to produce more copies than ever, but we communicate less and less. These are the times of fast foods and slow digestion, big men and small character, steep profits and shallow relationships. These are the days of two incomes but more divorce, fancier houses, but broken homes. These are days of quick trips, disposable diapers, throwaway morality, one night stands, overweight bodies, and pills that do everything from cheer, to quiet, to kill. It is a time when there is much in the showroom window and nothing in the stockroom. A time when technology can bring this letter to you, and a time when you can choose either to share this insight, or to just hit delete...Remember, spend some time with your loved ones, because they are not going to be around forever. Remember, say a kind word to someone who looks up to you in awe, because that little person soon will grow up and leave your side. Remember, to give a warm hug to the one next to you, because that is the only treasure you can give with your heart and it doesn't cost a cent. Remember, to say, 'I love you' to your partner and your loved ones, but most of all mean it. A kiss and an embrace will mend hurt when it comes from deep inside of you. Remember to hold hands and cherish the moment for someday that person will not be there again. Give time to love, give time to speak! And give time to share the precious thoughts in your mind. And always remember: Life is not measured by the number of breaths we take, but by the moments that take our breath away.

THE AUTHOR

 Raised in Providence, Rhode Island, Ari Newman is a film producer, lecturer, writer, amateur gourmet chef, and a community activist for which he was honored with the first Charlotte Bloomberg Award presented to him in 1993 by Mayor Michael Bloomberg. During his senior year at Boston University he produced his first feature film, *Squeeze*, which was nominated for an Independent Spirit Award and was purchased by Miramax Films.

His films have appeared at countless international film festivals, including the Sundance Film Festival, at which *Next Stop Wonderland* was purchased by Miramax Films for one of the largest sums ever paid for a Sundance film. In the United States he released *All My Loved Ones* starring Rupert Graves as Nicholas Winton, the stockbroker who organized the Kindertransport which saved the lives of over 600 children during World War 2 and was Slovakia's official Best Foreign Language Film submission to the 72nd Academy Awards. His most famous film is *National Lampoon's Van Wilder* considered by many to be Ryan Reynolds break out film.

UNCERTAINTY is his third book in three years. In early March 2017 he released his first book, AMERICA FIRST: A Modern Fable, a story about a modern day civil war, which became the first book to have been both written and published after the 2017 Presidential Inauguration. His second novel is a series titled MRS. VANDERBILT (Volume I - *Primogeniture*) that was released in November 2018. It is an alternate history novel series set during the Gilded Age that introduces America's first royal family, their great rivalry with the Astors, and the story of three heiresses only one of whom is destined to be crowned "Mrs. Vanderbilt."

Ari lives in the holy city of Jerusalem, Israel with his dog Carlos.

www.ingramcontent.com/pod-product-compliance
Lightning Source LLC
Chambersburg PA
CBHW050756250626
47155CB00005B/2093